The Leftover World
Memoirs from a Parallel Universe
Universe 54261 X 10^∞
by
Lawrence BoarerPitchford

The Leftover World

Memoirs from a Parallel Universe

Lawrence BoarerPitchford

Published by Lawrence BoarerPitchford, 2024.

THE LEFTOVER WORLD

First edition. June 1, 2024.

Copyright © 2024 Lawrence BoarerPitchford.

ISBN: 979-8988041733

Written by Lawrence BoarerPitchford.

Table of Contents

Foreword

Humans are not without the appearance of contentment. But oftentimes, things happen to them and around them—things that become apocalyptic. It is a universal truth that all beings wonder how or why; it is a question formed deep within their consciousness and a thought that will scribe a permeant mark upon their lives as they live them. Yet, it is the nature of the human animal to relish the suffering—the suffering of those around it—especially of its own kind. So, in the twilight of our age, know that those called men and women, the male and female of the human species, flee their towers and congested spaces from fear of creeping death; dwell by the rivers; and seek food from the cold, hard woodlands. And thus is sowed into the furrows of history the ranks of a once-great and powerful society cast into oblivion. Do not seek an answer to that poignant question of how or why. Just know that suffering for humans will never change. As a species, humans will never curb their hate, greed, or cruelty, and for the good of the universe, let us see that species fade from the great void and be forgotten.

– From the journal of Emeril Donley, the last to have seen the fall of the cities

Chapter 1

The Harvest

THE OXCART STOPPED, and Dallas got off. From end to end, Scatter Town was a little less than a half mile long. Dallas looked upon the grotesque lumps of twisted metal, broken wood, and heaps of rubble. These piles were old, for the metal that protruded was heavily rusted and the wood a light gray and splintered. Among the ancient lumps, sprung up like mushrooms in a forest, an array of buildings still stood, but barely. They were occupied by the citizens of the town based on each person's specialty: a tinker, a blacksmith, farm laborers, and those managing the perishable stored goods. Each building sported a shingle that hung down over the door that advertised, with a painted picture, the skill that person offered.

Thick dust choked every inch of the burg. Dallas was entranced by it all, for it was the first time he'd been allowed off the ranch to venture into the formidable regions of the world. Questions grew in his mind as he looked upon the town and the muddy street that ran down the middle of it.

He drew in a breath. The sweet smell of watercress, mint, and cattails wafted upon the air from the irrigation ditches. "Main Street," Dallas said, pointing at the faded green sign affixed atop a rusted metal pole.

"Ya, Dallas. That's what it reads like. Now don't dally about. The minders done chose us to do a right and proper task, such as bring in this harvest. Mind your questions and load the wagon with the supplies. We need to be back to the ranch before they come a looking for us," William said.

Dallas walked down the dusty street. He worked his mouth and tongue about as he smelled some sort of meat cooking among the structures. But the red dust that came with the delicious scent graced his tongue instead. He cringed. "Like licking an old iron pan," he mumbled.

"What was that?" William asked while glancing over at Dallas.

"Nothing..."

Dallas stopped at another rusted pole, this one much thicker. It had a high bar that sat crossways over the road. Stretching down from the middle of it was a rectangle with dirt-caked circles down the center.

"What's that thing?" Dallas asked.

William snapped the reins and moved the cart along the street. "Something from before the fall I guess. None of our concern now. Come on. Let's get those sacks and jars. I don't want to be taken off this job and put working the mines or the mill—or worse."

Dallas shrugged and followed the cart. He was used to being told to shut up and do as he was told. Questions on the ranch were reserved for immediate information regarding work, and that was all. But he couldn't help it; thoughts of what lay beyond the hills and rivers of the Turbulent Lands filled his imagination.

He looked up at William, a handsome boy with stringy blond hair, a broad jaw, and a slightly upturned nose. He was getting close to Turnout, the time he might be sold to a town, mine works, or a plantation. Though neither William nor Dallas knew their exact ages, the age of Turnout, it was said, was seventeen, and Dallas had heard a minder say that William was getting close.

Dallas had been brought to the ranch by a clan of child catchers when he'd just turned old enough to walk and speak. His mother and father had lain in their bedroom, dead from some sickness. He had lingered at the broken-down shack for two days before the catchers had come. The cart already had several children in it; Dallas watched them through a knot hole in the wall.

The catchers had searched the property, dragged out the bodies of his parents, and found him hiding behind a chest with a blanket over his head. He'd cried the whole journey to the ranch. The other children had only watched him, their dark, sunken, terror-filled eyes and hollow cheeks telling a sad tale of hunger and neglect.

Once at the ranch, he'd been exchanged for supplies, and the catchers, with their empty cart, had left down the road. He and the other kids watched the craft vanish over a grass covered hill, then the minder shouted at them, and they were herded into the reception room. There, heads were shaved, and clothes taken and burned. Baths were given and ranch attire issued. After, orders were barked at them from every direction, and never stopped.

William, a few years older than Dallas, was the closest thing to a brother he had since coming to the ranch.

"Dallas!" called William from down the street. "Come on. You're gona put us behind schedule!"

Dallas shook himself from his memories and ran to catch up with the cart. He came to a halt at a brick-and-cement structure with a rusty tin roof. The building, the town's storehouse, seemed the only thing still defiant against the elements. Years of dust and rain had caked the reddish-dark dirt to the walls, and flakes of red paint still clung to the tarnished metal door, yet the structure remained solid.

William got off the wagon and slammed his fist against the portal.

"Coming!" called a woman's voice from the other side.

The door opened, and a matronly-looking older woman carrying a rifle looked out. "William?"

"Yup."

"I suppose you've come for the supplies?"

"Yes, ma'am."

"Around the back at the loading dock," she responded. "Next time, just pull up there." She closed the door and locked it.

"Come on," William said to Dallas.

A few minutes later, the cart was snug up against a thick cement landing with a ramp. The woman opened the metal sliding door.

"The things for you are stacked by the water barrel," the woman told them.

Both boys went inside; carried out the sacks of flour, tins of lard, and small bags of salt; and put them in the wagon. A crate of vegetables and fruits followed. Finally, they fetched large containers of milk and stacked them at the end of the wagon. Once the goods were loaded, William tied them with some rope and got back up on the seat.

"What happened to the other boys who used to fetch the supplies?" the woman asked.

"They done sold them to the farm at Derby Town down in Hampton." William smiled. "Thanks for the supplies."

The lady nodded. "Don't get out of line, boys. Safe journey back." She turned and went back in. "See you in a couple of weeks," she said over her shoulder as the door locked shut.

THE OXCART WENT UP and down the rolling hills. The road was straight, broken only by various metal gates and long fences that trailed off into the distance on either side.

Opening the gates was like a game for Dallas. William stopped the cart. Dallas jumped down, opened the wooden barrier, and then closed it after the cart rolled on. He'd run after the buckboard, leap onto the back, and then scramble up onto the front seat to wait for the next gate.

"William? What do you know about the fall of the cities?"

"Why you always asking questions, Dallas?" William shook his head.

"Don't rightly know. When I see things, my head makes the questions."

"Well, I don't know much," said William. "I'm told way back when, people were really wicked and was doing all sorts of bad stuff."

"Like what kind of bad stuff?"

William shrugged. "You know, Dallas... Bad things like stealing, killeen, and naughty things. Then one day, they started to die."

"Like my mom and da?" Dallas asked.

"I don't know nothing about that," William replied. "I think the fall all happened long, long ago. I heard first there were a few in the cities that lay down dead, then more, and finally thousands died in heaps."

Dallas cocked his head to the side. "Thousands? There isn't that many people in the world."

William chuckled. "Maybe not. But what I do know is that you got a lot to learn."

Dallas jumped from the cart, ran in front, and threw open the coming gate. William coaxed the ox and cart through. Dallas closed it then climbed up and sat next to William again.

"What killed all those folks?" Dallas asked.

"The wrath of God. They was wicked, remember?"

Dallas nodded. "If God smites the wicked, why doesn't he smite the minders?"

"Don't talk like that, or you'll get both our hides on the strapper," William chided.

Dallas nodded and then turned to see the dark orange sky as the sun dipped beyond the hills. "One day I'll be a farmer...maybe," he said, a wispy sound to his voice.

"The only way either of us will get on a farm is if we get sold to one. Until then, we're just hands doing work," William reminded Dallas.

"I know. But maybe one day we'll not be just hands, or sold, but run away from the ranch."

"Don't talk like that!" William scolded. "The minders hear you say something like that, they'll put you in the clinker. Don't even think it." William's voice was impassioned.

Dallas nodded then looked ahead as the road snaked up and over the rolling hills.

Darkness descended as the sun fell farther behind the mountains. The oxcart was on the incline along the old road, which still occasionally showed the dark black surface and yellow lines between the patches of grass and among the wheel tracks.

"Look, William. That yellow and black. What is it?" Dallas asked.

"Damned if I know. Maybe one day you'll find out."

"Them wicked souls were crafty to make a road of black with yellow," Dallas said.

"Forget them oldies. They are gone from the world. Think about us and where we are and what we got'a do. Don't let your dreaming get us both strapped or in the clinker." William looked over and put his arm around Dallas's shoulders. "Just keep doing right, and we'll be okay."

The stars were beginning to take their place in the heavens. The flickering white glow of the ranch gate lamp was visible through the trees. They'd be at the ranch soon, and though Dallas was not in trouble, the feeling in his chest made him feel as if he was.

From an early age, he'd earned the ire of a few of the minders. More than once, he'd received a beating for a minor offense. One time, he'd been left unable to move for a few days, and he'd had to rest in the infirmary. "An example," one of the minders, Burk, had called him.

William slowed the ox as they approached the gates to the ranch. "Open the gate!" he shouted.

Two men with rifles appeared from behind the brick gateposts. One slid the latch and pulled the gate outward. The lane was uphill. William moved the cart in, and then the first access gate closed behind them.

Just ahead was a second gate, and one of the men went over, unlocked it, and pulled it open. He lifted his rifle and lay it upon his shoulder as William passed.

"Glad to see you boys back. Another hour and we'd have to mount up and come looking for ya," he said.

"Hope ya didn't eat none of the groceries. That means a beating if ya did!" the other man shouted after William and Dallas.

Dallas looked down at the long inner perimeter fence topped with razor wire. It was old, rusted, and leaning in places, but it served to secure the ranch and all its occupants from skulkers, raiders, and raggers. *Any one of those types get in, and bloody trouble will commence,* Dallas thought.

Dallas looked up at the watchtower. Armed men looked out from the open windows. A few weeks back, he had seen one of those men from the tower bag a wild dog. A minder had retrieved it, and the cook had served up some of the meat for the wards. It had been greasy, stringy, and gamey but a sight better than the stewed oats or millet they typically got.

The cart rolled up and onto a level road. The social house was one of the structures in a long line of buildings along the street. A lantern hung over the door, illuminating the entrance. Some of the minders were coming out of the building. A few looked drunk. They followed the cart to the storehouse and then helped unload the cargo.

"Dallas, come here!" Burk barked.

Dallas immediately moved to where Burk was standing. Without a word, Burk cuffed Dallas and knocked him to the ground.

The brute staggered and nearly fell too. He stood up as straight as he could and looked at the other minders. "See, this kid can take wrap to the puss." He laughed.

Trev, the lead minder, rushed over and stood between Dallas and Burk. "Burk, you thick-headed shit! Leave off the boy. He got'a work in the morning, and whacking him is just going to pile up the workload for all."

Burk flushed red and balled his fist. "Trev, you ain't oughta speak to me like that. You might be top minder, but you ain't in this fight."

Trev's eyes appeared to glow with violence. "Watch that mouth of yours, Burk, or I'll put you at the boot end of a shit kicking. The boss done made me top dog, and top I'll stay. And until I'm not anymore, you do as I say! Or you can take your tack and blanket and get back on that lonely road down there."

Burk wobbled back and then looked down the hill past the fence and into the darkness. He snapped back, steadied himself, and stared hard at Trev. "I ain't going anywhere." He walked around Trev and then tried to kick Dallas but missed. "Pish! You little nothing! You'll rot one day—rot in the ground like the rest." He walked off toward the bunkers.

"You okay, kid?" Trev reached down and helped Dallas up.

Dallas rubbed his jaw. "No worse than usual."

"One day I hope you kids flay that shit alive," he whispered.

Dallas remained quiet. He knew better than to speak his mind while at the ranch. There were much worse things that could happen to him than just being struck to the ground.

"Get you both back to the dorms. I'll stable the ox and take care of the cart," Trev said.

"You sure, Mister Trev?" William asked just to make sure he wouldn't get in trouble for leaving the cart or the ox to someone else.

"Ya," Trev said. "You don't have to worry about it tonight. You boys did a bang-up job. We was right to choose you two to bring in the harvest."

William nodded and then smiled at Dallas. "Come on. Let's see if there's any food left in the kitchen."

Dallas and William headed along a cement path that wound its way up the hill toward a large stone building. William stopped at the black metal door and knocked.

"Who's there?" The door came open.

"Dodgy!" William said, his voice filled with respect.

"Eh! It's you boys. Well, come in. I've kept some porridge hot for you both and some clean water to drink."

William and Dallas went in. Dodgy led them to a wooden table set with two bowls and two glasses of water. He came over with a pot, ladled out some porridge into each dish, and sat down with them.

Dallas's stomach growled loudly as he shoveled a big spoonful into his mouth.

"Slow down, son. That stuff will give ya nightmares if you eat it too fast," Dodgy said.

Dallas nodded and tempered his ferocity. The food was bland but filling. He was thankful that old Dodgy was so kind.

"Dodgy, how old are you now?" asked William.

"Let me see," Dodgy began. "Sixty-two years come this winter."

"Did you ever see any of the wicked folks from the city?" Dallas asked.

Dodgy chuckled. "The city folk? I ain't never seen no city folks living. They all died out after the fall. Wait! Come to think of it, I did see one. His old, boney, white skull come up out of the ground when I was plowing some years ago." He emitted a hearty guffaw. "But I don't think that's quite what you meant."

"How'd they die?" Dallas asked, almost spilling some of the porridge from his mouth.

"All I know is what the preachers done told me. When the fire and darkness came, those who hid in the ground lived, and those who didn't fell to the scythe of the giant reaper."

"What was the fire and darkness?" Dallas furthered.

"Fire is fire, boy. It burns the skin from yer bones. The darkness? None really know," Dodgy said. "All I was ever told was that them in the wicked cities began dying. Then, as scriptures say, the fires came and turned those in cities to ash, and the sky turned dark even when the sun were out. Only God saved our old fathers, guiding them to the forests and farms, and sent the wicked to the dark realms of the void."

Dallas finished his meal and drank down his water.

Dodgy picked up their dishes. "I'll take care of these. You boys get off to your bunks. Morning will come soon'nuf and y'all get the chance to work off any breakfast you get by turning it into sweat." Dodgy snickered as he went to the kitchen basin and started cleaning the plates.

Chapter 2

Lost on the Way

DALLAS WOKE. IT WAS still dark. The cool air came in through the open window, the lingering smell of spring filled his nose, and crickets and tree frogs chirped loudly outside. He sat up in his bunk and dangled his feet over the edge.

Looking down, he saw his dormmate still asleep. Vic always slept in until the first morning bell rang.

Dallas jumped down and went to the pitcher on the small wooden table. He poured some water into the terracotta basin, washed his face, and put on his clothes and boots.

Clanging erupted. "Up, up, up, you curs!" shouted someone from outside. "Time to earn your bread!"

Dallas rushed down the stairs, used the latrine, and then dashed over to the mess before the line was too long. Those who were late often went hungry in the early hours of a working day.

Once fed, Dallas reported to the roll-call line for his daily work detail. He stood there waiting patiently as the line grew in numbers. Mister Ugert, Trev, and Burk stood waiting.

In the distance, the second bell rang.

"You, you, and you!" Burk pointed at three boys. "Report to Weshly Farm." He moved down the line, assigning and shouting. As he came to Dallas, he stopped, gave him a hard look, then grinned wickedly. "Calvine Mill." He let out a malevolent chuckle.

No one wanted Calvine Mill. It was rumored that the overseer there liked young boys. Dallas had heard fearful stories of that place.

Burk picked out three others to work at the mill.

"Move out!" Mister Ugert yelled.

Dallas moved down the hill, following the other three to the inner fence west gate. There a minder opened the portal and allowed them to leave along a well-trodden dirt path.

The boys were quiet as they moved in single file to the second fence and through that gate. It was only a few minutes before they entered the woods. A few miles away, at the end of that path, was the Ether River and, on its banks, the Calvine Mill with its large waterwheel churning all day and night.

Tommy, who was at the front, stopped. They all stopped. Turning, he wore the serious look of someone desperate. "Look," he began, "if we stick together and don't let any of our workmates go off with that overseer, we'll be okay. Somehow, we each need to find a way to be there if he tries to take one of us off."

They each swore an oath to protect the other. Once Tommy was satisfied, he turned on his heels and set off again.

It took an hour to reach the mill. Once they arrived, a lanky fellow who had short blond hair, wore a white apron, and held a truncheon at his side met them at the main gate.

"Mmm." The man's lips turned upward at the corners. "The miller will be pleased. Don't believe you've come here before. We'll have to think of a way to thank Burk for his thoughtful choices." He led them into the mill house, where great wheels of stone were crushing grain into flour. It was dusty and noisy. "You boys are lucky you didn't get sent to the mines. You're lucky you got me to watch over you. I help you, you help me. That's how it works here. I'm Carter, the miller's assistant." The man's voice was odd, tense, and filled with anxiety. "Who among you is the oldest?"

Tommy raised his hand.

"Okay. You're in charge of the rest. I don't want no accidents, and if there's trouble, come get me fast. Now I'll show you what needs to be done." Carter pointed to a large burlap sack of grain. "Pick that up and carry it up the ladder. You'll have to work to get it up by the hopper. Pour it into the large vessel above the spinning disk of stone. Mind your hands, head, and feet. I don't want no injuries. Now, get this work done. I'll be up at the miller's house if you need me." Carter headed for the door, stopped, and turned back. "If you're good, you might even get some pie. Oh, I'll be coming back from time to time to take you to meet the miller. He really likes to meet the young ones...take the measure of those working for him, as it were." Carter leered at the boys, then vanished through the shadow of the doorway and into the unyielding light outside.

Tommy looked at the others. "Okay, we know his trick. He'll try and single one of us out to go see the miller. Dallas, you get up the ladder with Jon. Terry and I will lift the grain sacks up to you. We'll try and be too busy to go see the miller when he comes back."

"What if he gets one of us and we have to go?" Terry asked.

"One of us will head to the house and make up something about one of us getting hurt, being sick, or something," Tommy said.

"Which one of us?" Terry asked.

Tommy looked at Dallas, Jon, and Terry. "I guess it'll have to be me." The relieved looks on the others' faces told him that he'd said something they all agreed with.

Tommy and Terry pushed the first sack of grain up the ladder. Dallas and Jon pulled it up, cut the top with a hook knife, and dumped the contents into the hopper. This went on for a good couple of hours. Then, just before midday, Carter returned.

"The miller wants to see"—he looked around—"you." Carter pointed at Jon.

Jon looked at Tommy.

"Don't worry, boys. He'll be back shortly," Carter told them.

Jon looked at the others with apprehension. "Tommy?" he implored.

"Hey!" Carter shouted, his face turning a scalding red. "The miller ain't got all day for waiting."

"It'll be okay," Tommy said to Jon.

Jon looked a bit relieved. "Okay," he said and followed Carter out of the millhouse.

As they worked, Tommy went to the entrance and looked out along the gravel road. This occurred a few times, and then he swallowed hard and looked at his friends. "Dallas, you and Terry keep working. I'm going to tell em we got an injury. Dallas, you be ready to limp when we come back." He left out the riverside door.

Terry and Dallas looked at one another, then went back to work. One after another, they hauled the grain bags from the stack, up the ladder, and into the grinder.

The shadows outside were vanishing as the lunch break approached. Terry looked toward the door. "Tommy should have been back by now."

"Should we go see?" Dallas asked.

"Screw this. Follow me," Terry said.

They both left by the river door.

Outside, the sun was driving the heat up. Great oaks hung over the road, leading up and over the hillside. The air by the river was cool, dewy. They moved along the bank and up into the thick brush. The miller's house, a two-story whitewashed structure, was on a stone ledge overlooking the river. A garden lay just beyond a faded white picket fence. No birds chirped, and no animals made noise in the woods surrounding the house. Dark windows watched them, their shadowed reflections brooding in the silence.

Both boys crouched and moved quickly to the fence and then into the yard. Dallas approached the window and peeked in. Tommy was lying prone on the floor, some blood on the side of his head. From the second floor, there came a muffled cry, and then it was quiet.

Terry went to a side door and lifted the latch. Inside smelled of smoke and dust. An anguished cry came from upstairs. Terry grabbed a wrought iron fire poker, lifted it high, and looked at Dallas.

Dallas looked about for a weapon. Near the corner of the room, propped up against the wall, was a rifle. He'd used one when Trev had taken him hunting the year before, so he knew how to use it and exactly what it could do. Next to the gun was an open rolltop desk with ammunition in a faded red box tucked against the side. He picked up the firearm, quickly loaded a few rounds into the magazine, and then quietly locked a bullet into the chamber.

Slowly, they climbed the steps. At the top was a hallway. They crept forward. Terry stopped at an open door and did a quick peek inside the room. He looked back at Dallas, held up two fingers, and then charged in swinging the poker.

"What the fuck are you doing in here?" a voice in the room yelled.

There was a crash, a thud, and then a moaning cry. Dallas rushed in.

Jon was tied over a barrel. His pants were down. Terry was fighting with Carter, trying to smash him in the head with the poker. A fair amount of blood dribbled down the man's face. There was another man with a baton in his hand, ready to deliver a blow to Terry.

Without hesitation, Dallas leveled the rifle and fired. There was a crack in the air; smoke spewed out toward the man; and he fell back with a cry, clutching his chest, blood pumping between his fingers. He fell onto the white and cornflower blue cushions of a window seat and lay still, the crimson liquid pooling beneath him.

Carter let go of Terry and rushed past Dallas through the door in a panic. At the top of the stairs, Dallas fired. Carter cried out, tumbled headfirst down the steps, and landed in a crumpled heap at the bottom.

Tommy appeared, one hand clutching the hand railing and the other pressing a bloody cloth against his head wound. "What did you two do?" he shouted as he looked down at Carter's body.

Terry and Jon came from the bedroom. Jon's eyes were red from crying.

"They didn't get him," Terry said. "He's okay." His legs became wobbly, and he leaned against the wall as the blood drained from his face.

"What do we do now?" Dallas asked Tommy.

Tommy looked up at Dallas and then down at Carter's body again. "I don't know. But what I do know is that if we go back to the ranch, they'll chop us up and feed us to the pigs!"

"What do we do then?" Dallas repeated.

"Come on. Let's get this guy into the river," Tommy said.

"There's another up here," Terry stated.

"Okay, okay. We dump both in the river," Tommy replied. "Then we clean up the blood."

"Then what?" Jon asked.

"I don't know." Tommy pressed the rag against his head.

"We got'a run for it," Dallas stated.

"The minders will be on our trail by tonight when we don't arrive back at the ranch," Tommy argued.

"You said it, Tom. They's back at the ranch...they have to deal with this, and they will do so by strapping our hides until we have none left," Terry said, the color returning to his cheeks.

"Let's get them into the river, then we'll decide on what more to do," Tommy told them.

It was a struggle, but they got both bodies into the river and watched them float away. All four boys returned to the miller's house. The blood was getting sticky, and they scrubbed most of it off with a bucket of water, a stiff brush, and soap.

Tommy and Jon came up the stairs to check on Dallas and Terry. "Get it all cleaned up?" Tommy asked.

Dallas shrugged. "I got most of the blood off the floor, but the pillows in the window-."

There was a shout outside.

"Hey! Carter? Where you at? Where are those boys? They ain't in the mill. You ain't doing the four of them all at once, are you?"

It was the voice of Burk. All four boys remained still. They heard the door downstairs open.

"You up there?" Burk shouted into the house.

All four boys were frozen with fear. Dallas steeled his resolve. He crept to the corner of the doorway and leveled the rifle at the top of the stairs.

"Where the void did you go?" shouted Burk.

The door slammed, and footsteps trailed away outside.

Jon went to the second-floor window. "He's heading back toward the mill."

Tommy looked panicked. "We got to get out of here now!"

All four went downstairs. Dallas stopped at the spot where he'd picked up the gun, and he grabbed the remaining rifle cartridges. They rushed out the back door and into the woods. A few hundred yards out, they stopped to catch their breath.

"Now what?" Jon asked.

"We got'a get to someplace where we can figure out what to do," Tommy said. "That's the Ether River, and about twenty miles that way is Scatter Town, where we get the supplies."

"It's all open farmland out that way," Terry said. "No place to hide if someone spots us."

"That's the only place I can think of that is any somewhere we can hide for the night," Tommy told them. "All agreed?"

Dallas put the rifle on his shoulder the way Trev had taught him. "I agree."

Jon and Terry nodded.

The path they took was winding. They crossed the river a few times. After an hour, they emerged onto a vast treeless plain. All around were green, growing-waist-high wheat and barley.

Beyond, the waves of grass crashed into long furrows of cabbages, carrots, turnips, potatoes, and beets.

They moved slowly, crouching or sometimes lying down when distant farmhands would look up from their hoeing or digging, or working along the irrigation ditches.

Scatter Town was not too far now. A few miles and they'd see the outline of the village. Tommy kept the lead, avoiding the scant field hands galumphing about. And every so often, he'd look back the way they had come.

As the sun was setting, the four boys reached the edge of town. In the air was the smell of baking bread and roasting meats and veggies. In the distance, there were voices chatting about the day.

They hid by a pile of rubble, one of the old buildings that had succumbed to the elements and age.

Tommy led them along a dark shadow that lay like a scar across the town's Main Street. As Dallas crossed, he cast a glance up at the strange dangling rectangle suspended in midair.

Terry reached out and grabbed Tommy's shoulder. "If the minders done got the hounds, they'll be coming for us soon."

Tommy looked up at the darkening sky. "By now they know we ain't coming back. We crossed the river, and I ain't seen no hound that can track over water. Come on."

He led the way to an abandoned building and around the back. The splintering wood door was ajar, and he pushed it open just enough for them to enter. Inside was dark, and the smell of dust and mold was strong. "Looks like there ain't no one living in here," he said to the others. "Find a spot to sit and I'll be right back."

They all entered the ramshackle structure. Once inside, they found a few places on the floor to lie down. The dust and dirt inside seemed as plentiful as it was outside in the streets.

Each lad cleared a place and nestled in. Dallas found a spot by some piled-high wooden crates and boxes filled with junk. He tried looking through one of the big dirt-coated windows at the front, but in the dark, he couldn't see anything in the street outside.

Tommy returned. "I ain't seen no one looking for us. Most of the townies are taking the evening meal. I'll keep a watch for a few hours, then Terry, Dallas, and finally Jon. Now try and get some sleep. We be on the run now and need as much rest as we can get."

Dallas was in a deep sleep when Terry woke him. "Your turn," Terry whispered.

Dallas nodded and then rubbed his eyes. All around, the walls emitted a subtle green glow. Dallas waited for Terry to nod off and then moved carefully around the room. The windows were filthy. *Probably never cleaned since the fall of the cities*, he thought. There was a raised counter made of some strange material—hard like stone but smooth like glass.

As he weaved his way between crates and boxes, he heard the clop of hooves. Somewhere nearby, a person began shouting.

"Runaways! Runaways are at large!" the man yelled.

A commotion began, and as people were coming into the street, their lanterns looked like fuzzy orange orbs floating outside the filthy windows.

Dallas woke Terry, Tommy, and Jon. "There's something happening outside," he whispered.

"What's this all about?" a man demanded.

"Some boys done ran off the ranch! There's a reward for their capture. They done killed the miller and his apprentice. We found them down the river, both shot," the messenger detailed.

"Do you know where they went?" asked another man.

"The dogs tracked them to the river but lost the scent—for now. They're still looking."

"We'll keep an eye out here and send a messenger to the ranch if we see 'em," the local man said.

"Spread the word to any outlanders who come to trade. They're four boys named Tommy, Terry, Dallas, and Jonny. Whoever turns them in will get a free month of labor from the ranch."

The clopping of hooves echoed along the street.

"What'da we do, Carl?" asked a different male voice.

"Go back to bed. If them boys is dumb enough to come here, we'll slap the shackles on 'em. If they're spotted around here, we'll hunt 'em down," Carl stated.

The torches and lanterns floated away into the dark as the footsteps faded. The boys remained silent, listening for anyone approaching. After a time, they each lay down again.

"Before first light, we got to get out of here," Tommy said. "Dallas, keep watch, and wake Jon when it's his turn." He turned to Jon. "Wake us all before first light so we can slip out of here before them townies find us."

Chapter 3

Daybreak

DALLAS SLOWLY OPENED his eyes. A dull muted light was coming in from the windows. He climbed to a sitting position and froze. A shadowy figure was standing there. He felt his heart leap into his throat.

As his eyes adjusted, he saw a girl in a flowery dress, boots, and work gloves. She was silent as she brushed her dark bangs from her eyes.

"You the boys that done run off the ranch?" she asked.

Tommy, Terry, and Jon sat up and stared.

"You ain't got no worries with me," she said. "My mom says they at the ranch are keepers of slaves, and we don't believe in slavery." She looked at each boy then smiled. "I also heard rumors about the miller." Her eyes tracked across each boy's face. "My name is Sheela. I won't turn you in. Stay here and I'll bring you some food. This old building is used for keeping scarp and junk. No one comes here these days. Keep quiet and no one will know you're here."

Dallas nodded. Sheela turned and left quietly.

Tommy looked over at Dallas. "Go to the door and watch. If she's bringing men, we'll need to get out of here fast." He looked at Jon. "Why didn't you wake us? Did you fall asleep?"

Jon looked down at his feet. "I tried to keep my eyes open, but I suppose I fell asleep. Sorry, Tommy."

Dallas went to the door. The morning light was casting long shadows toward the west. The smell of the crops and irrigation water hung heavy in the air. Around the corner of the far building came Sheela. She carried a pot with some bowls tied to the top. Her manner of walking was carefree and bubbly.

"Sheela!"

A man wearing coveralls and carrying a rifle approached her. "Where you going with that food?" he asked.

"Now, Carl Write, you know that I take a little bit of extra food out to the West family from time to time. They're in need, and we got a little more than we can eat. Plus, since Mister West done came down with the sick, he can't get no food from hunting." Sheela smiled and dangled the pot by its handle.

"You be careful. There be four young men escaped from the ranch, and they are armed. If you see anything, let me know right away!" Carl looked around at the buildings and then walked off between two.

Sheela stood there for a few minutes. She then set the pot down, adjusted her dress, and brushed it with her hands. She looked around, picked up the pot again, and skipped over to the building where the boys were hiding. She looked around once more and then slipped in through the door, driving Dallas backward into the room.

Dallas's feet became tangled in an open box, but he caught himself before falling. Sheela looked at him with a grin and a giggle.

"Careful. Them sheriffs about and looking to take you boys back to the ranch. Here." She handed Dallas the pot. "Stay hidden until midday when the lunch horn blows, then slip out and head northwest. There's a deep watering ditch there. The farm workers will be eating their midday meal, and you won't be seen. Follow the canal as far as Burly Hills, then take the old road toward the fallen city. Mind the big cave at the end. The irrigation water comes from there. I ain't never been in it, but it looks scary.

"When you're done with the pot, just put it outside. I'll come pick it up when I'm done taking food to the workers." Sheela turned and left the building.

The boys circled around the pot, took bowls, and began ladling out helpings into each container. They ate quickly without conversation. When done, they stacked the bowls inside the pot and put it by the doorway.

Dallas looked out from the shadows. The sun was nearly overhead. They'd waited a couple of hours and were all getting edgy. The day was growing late and warm when a horn blared outside. As they waited, they heard people walking past the old building.

"This is it," Tommy said. "The midday meal."

Food was being cooked somewhere beyond the dilapidated buildings. The smell was growing more tantalizing. Jon's stomach growled.

"Come on," Tommy said and led them out the door and toward the north of town. A few farm workers were straggling in from the furrows, hoes over their shoulders, chatting to each other as they walked, their eyes watching their feet to make sure they didn't trip over a row, rock, or dirt clod.

The last building had partially collapsed. It had once been large. The faded painting of a falcon was on the side. They hid by a pile of rubble, then when the coast was clear, they moved out into the fields and toward the westerly hills.

After a few minutes, they went down into a wide cement ditch partially filled with water. No one could see them in the canal.

The sides were angled toward the water, making it hard for them to run, but they made good time anyway. By late afternoon, they were approaching the massive hole belching water from the side of the mountain into the channel.

Up along the growing hills were poplar and birch trees. Dallas smelled the sweet scent of the bark.

Tommy investigated the conduit. "It's dark in there. If we go in, we'll need some sort of light."

"Come on. Let's take a break inside. It's cool, and no one will see us in the dark of the tunnel," Terry said.

Tommy thought for a moment. "Okay. But when it gets dark, we'll start climbing up the hill and make for the top."

Dallas climbed up inside the culvert. His feet were submerged up to his shins as he moved through the crystal-clear water into the darkness. Twenty feet in, they came to a metal trestlework, an elevated catwalk along the side of the flowing water.

"Hey. There's a path that gets us up and out of the water." Dallas climbed up the ladder and onto the walkway.

Each boy climbed up and moved down the metal path a few dozen feet. Tommy sat facing the opening. The great oval was choked with golden sunlight.

Some time passed as the boys quietly discussed their strategy for further flight.

"The only place that I know of is Whistle Town, and it's more than three days from..." Tommy grew quiet as a shadow hovered at the opening to the conduit.

A human shape appeared—a black outline against the light of the day.

"Are you guys in here?" Sheela called.

Dallas stood up, got into the water, and waded back toward the entrance. The others saw him silhouetted by the light.

"How did you find us?" Dallas asked, a modicum of concern in his voice.

"I told you where to go, remember?" Sheela said. "I brought you some things. Here's a backpack with a week's worth of dried food, a lantern, and some matches. There's a knife in there and a few pans too. That's all I could get without drawing any suspicion." She sat down at the edge where the water spilled into the canal. "Where you boys going to go?"

"Not sure. Maybe Whistle Town," Dallas said.

"Don't go there. The sheriff has sent runners to every nearby settlement telling them you're murderers." Sheela picked a yellow flower growing near the tunnel. "What's your name?"

Dallas's eyes widened, and he smiled shyly. "Dallas."

"I like you, Dallas." Sheela grinned. "I got'a head back to town before anyone misses me. Can I give you a kiss?"

Dallas felt weird—sort of like when he was in trouble, but not exactly. "Okay," he said.

She stood up on a rock next to the culvert and leaned into Dallas, who suddenly felt hot, and then she pressed her lips against his. His heart was beating hard. She pulled away and smiled again.

"That was nice," Sheela said and then turned, crossed the opening, and climbed down onto the canal bank. Her horse was tied just a few yards away.

Dallas moved back into the dark of the tunnel, and then he heard the beating of hooves.

"Sheela!" called a stout, masculine voice. "What are you doing out here?"

Dallas peaked from the shadow of the tunnel. Three men on horses were there. The one wearing a camouflaged brush hat climbed off his horse and approached Sheela.

"I've been out for a ride," she replied. I wanted to dangle my feet in the ditch, so I stopped here."

"Why didn't you tell us you were going out?" the man demanded. "I told you those boys that killed the miller and his assistant are out here." His voice stopped abruptly. "You haven't seen those boys, have you?"

"Naw, Sheriff Write. I had some time before the dinner prep and decided to take a little ride."

The two men with the sheriff dismounted and began looking at the conduit spillway. They moved slowly down into the cement ditch and toward the tunnel.

Write looked Sheela over and then directed his attention to her saddle. "She ain't got nothing to give to them boys," he said. "Come on. Let's head up Broker's Pass. If them renegades are heading anywhere, it is probably toward Whistle Town!"

The two men stopped, turned, and went back to their horses. Write and the others turned their mounts, but Write looked back.

"Get you back to town. Don't come out here again until them boys is found or dead," Write told Sheela, then he spurred his horse and rode off into the woods, followed closely by the other two men.

Dallas saw Sheela exhale. She looked back at the opening, mounted her horse, and headed off southeast along the canal.

Sloshing his way back upstream, Dallas carried the pack to his friends. "We can't go to Whistle Town. Looks like everyone is thinking we're headed there."

Tommy looked on the verge of tears. "There ain't no place I know we can go then."

Dallas took out the lantern and looked back at the entrance. It looked clear. He lit a match and ignited the wick. "Come on." He shouldered the pack and the rifle and then set out along the catwalk. "We can decide when we come out the other side of this waterway."

"You're assuming that there is an other side," Jon said.

"Walking through this hole is better than sitting and feeling sorry for ourselves," Dallas replied. "Seems a good place to hold up if it's just a dead end anyway. Give us a chance to let the commotion die down out there."

"Okay," Tommy said. "Let's go."

They walked for quite a while. No light appeared from the way they'd come, and save for the eerie glow of the lantern, none could be seen the way they were going. A strong smell of cold, damp air filled their lungs as they moved along. Under their feet, the water flowed steadily.

From time to time, they came to places where the steel catwalk was rusty and broken. They climbed down into the cold water, traversed the gaps, and kept going.

For how long they traveled, none of them could tell. When their footsteps fell more slowly and their fatigue began to peak, they stopped.

Dallas took off the pack and put his rifle up against the railing. He took a jar of dried fruit from the pack, removed some, and handed the container to Tommy.

"I hope it's not far now to the end," Dallas said. He lay on his stomach, reached down to the flowing water, cupped his hands, and took a drink.

They sat there for a brief time, and then Dallas took up the pack and rifle. "Come on."

In the distance, a tiny pinprick of light appeared. With each footfall, the light grew larger.

"I can smell the watercress and mint from the outside," Jon said excitedly.

"No one exit the tunnel until we make sure there is no one out there waiting for us," Tommy said.

The exit was as large as the entrance. The metal catwalk ended twenty feet from the conduit's mouth, and the boys sloshed their way to the last of the shadow extending into the cavern. Slowly, their feet grew numb as they looked and listened. The sound of birds, the scurrying of small game, and the chirping of frogs were all they heard.

Tommy exited first. "You guys stay here. I'll come back to get you if the coast is clear."

They watched as Tommy slipped into the brush alongside the cement channel. He looked around, went up over the lip, and disappeared from sight.

The boys went back to the trestle to allow their waterlogged feet to dry. They chatted about what might be out there. The sunlight was fading, and it appeared to Dallas that it was being swallowed up by the darkness of the cave.

"Hey," Tommy called. "Come on."

The boys moved toward the opening, and each climbed out onto the cement embankment.

"I found a place we can shelter. It's not too far from here." Tommy took the lantern and led the way. Night was coming, and the cool air from the canal mixed with the dusty dry air of the spring day.

Tommy stopped. The lantern cast a fiery glow upon a hole in the broken turf. They pulled away some of the grass and dirt. "Look," he said.

It was a black surface covered with a yellow stripe. Dallas knew it was an old road.

"I spotted it back near the tunnel. It was hard to see even in the daylight, but I know how to follow it," Tommy bragged.

The sun faded, and the stars began to speckle the dark sky.

Tommy stopped at what appeared to be a depression in a grass covered berm. He went in first and then held the lantern at the entrance. "Come on. Dallas, give me that knife."

Dallas handed over the blade.

Tommy grinned. "Take the others inside and find a spot to sleep. I'm going to cut some brush and hide the hole better." He slipped outside and was swallowed by the dark.

Dallas took the lead, holding the lantern up. The passageway was narrow and appeared to have once been painted. There were doors every four of five paces, each with a metal number.

Holding the lantern with one hand and gripping the knob with the other, Dallas opened door sixteen. It appeared to be stuck at first, but he put his shoulder to it, and it gave way. The lantern illuminated a set of bunk beds, a counter, a room with strange things in it, and what appeared to be a door with a circular wheel affixed to the middle of it.

"Okay, I covered the entrance," Tommy said as he came into the room.

"What is this place?" Terry asked.

"What's in this room?" Jon asked as he poked his head into a small adjacent compartment.

"They only know in the void," Tommy said. "I found the hole earlier and checked these hidden rooms along the sides. Some of the doors don't open, and some have dirt in them. It's strange alright."

"Something from the fall?" Dallas asked.

"Who can say? Let's try and get some sleep." Tommy pushed the door until it was almost closed and then sat on the bed. "We'll move again in the morning."

Dallas put down the pack, set the lantern on the counter, and took out the jars of dried food. "Here's some jerky and some nuts. I think these are dried apricots."

They took the time to eat, and then once the jars were put back, Dallas set the rifle up against the wall, took what appeared to be a dusty towel from the small room, and laid it down on the floor. He curled up and fell into a deep sleep.

Dallas was on a boat in the middle of a river. All around, the sound of rushing water assaulted his ears. The conveyance was rocking back and forth. He was holding onto the saxboards.

In the bottom of the craft was blood, and it was starting to rise, covering his shoes. Fish were flopping all around. The waters were growing dark as tar. He held on. There was a scream, and from the black water leapt the miller, who grabbed onto Dallas' arm and tried to drag him into the churning liquid and down into the unforgiving void.

Dallas woke, sweat on his brow and heart pounding.

Tommy was using the toe of his shoe to nudge Dallas' shoulder. "Come on. Time to get going. It's light outside."

"Okay. I'm getting up. Got'a piss," Dallas said.

Dallas grabbed the rifle, opened the door, and followed the dim light to the exit. There, he parted the stacked brush, crossed the old road, and went behind a tree by the canal.

As he was doing his business, he glanced upstream and saw something that confused him. There was a strange shimmer of the plants and then the water. On finishing, he stalked down the embankment and scanned the surrounding area. Shaking his head, he wondered whether the lack of sleep was making him see things. Whatever it was, was now gone, if it had been anything at all.

As he headed back to the cave, he saw Tommy come out carrying the pack, followed by Terry. As soon as Jonny exited, a shot rang out. A plug of wood from a nearby tree flew into the air, and the boys began to run along the old road. Dallas crouched. A half dozen men came running along the road in pursuit. Dallas blinked; one of the men was Burk, and another was Trev.

Chapter 4

A Hard Lesson

TWO MINDERS WENT INTO the shelter where the boys had stayed the night. Dallas receded into the foliage and slowly made his way down the embankment of the canal. Crouching low, he dashed as fast as he could upstream. Halfway to the bridge, he slowed.

Rusted metal rods showed through the cement where the sides of the canal had eroded. Holding the rifle at the ready, Dallas crept over breaks, large rocks, and bushes along the edge.

"Leave off!" shouted Jon.

"Shut up, or I'll slap you down again," chided a minder.

"We got 'em cornered at the tubes just ahead!" yelled Burk.

Dallas got down on his belly by a bush. Ahead was a bridge—battered, broken with age, but still spanning the waterway.

Burk came out onto the crossing and waved over the other minder, who had Jon by the back of his shirt. The man shook Jon hard and then shoved him forward.

"We goin'a hide you boys for what you did," Burk said, malevolence in his voice. "If you're lucky, the boss might just have you sent to the mines after we get done with ya."

"Keep moving," the other minder told Jon as he continued to push him across the span.

Once the minders were across, Dallas moved forward and then slunk under the bridge. From there, he crossed the waterway and went up the other side. Moving away from the rushing water, he heard voices.

"Come on out of there, or we'll have to smoke you out."

It was the voice of Trev.

"You won't get punished until we know your side of the story and what happened," Trev called out.

Dallas moved slowly, like he'd learned on the hunt. Crouched, he maneuvered through the thick underbrush, holding a branch here and watching where his foot landed there.

He lay down and crawled on his stomach until he had a commanding view of five very large, rusted metal cylinders, each with a square opening at ground level. Holding the rifle at his side, he watched for any advantage he could give his friends.

"Okay, pile up some brush," Trev said.

A few of the minders came and put dry bows by one of the square holes. Trev kneeled, lit a match, blew a few times, and stood back. Smoke rose into the air. Fire licked the branches and slowly grew in strength.

The other minder fanned the flames, driving the smoke into the hole. White billows began streaming from the top of the twenty-foot-high metal cylinder.

Coughing erupted inside.

"Okay! We're coming out!" Tommy yelled. This was followed by more coughing. "Stop with the smoke!"

"Pull it away, fellas," Trev said.

The other minders used some branches to drag the flaming wood away from the hole. They doused the fire with water from a canteen and stood with rifles at the ready.

"If you got any guns, toss 'em out!" Trev shouted.

"We ain't got no guns!" Tommy yelled. "We're coming out now."

Terry came out first, followed by Tommy. Their cheeks and foreheads were dark from the soot.

"Give 'em a drink, boys," Trev said.

"No!" Burk shouted. "They don't get no comfort! You ain't treating them murdering sons a bitches like normal plebs," he challenged.

"Burk, you got no say in this. This be my job to do, and if you don't like it, get you hence back to the ranch and sulk like the bitter panty crank you are!" Trev told Burk. He turned to Tommy.

A shot echoed, and Dallas blinked at the sound. Trev fell forward and lay still on the ground. A piece of his head was missing, and blood pooled around his cheek and shoulder.

"Burk, you dumb shit! What did you do?" one of the minders cried out, shock written across his face.

"What needed to be done, boys. Now, I'm in charge, and as far as you blokes are concerned, these renegades done shot ole Trev," Burk instructed them. "Now, tie these boys up, hands behind their backs. I got some ideas as to what to do to them over the next few days as we head back to the ranch!"

Dallas pulled the rifle up, put the butt on his shoulder, and leveled the weapon at Burk. His finger was squeezing down on the trigger. Tears formed in his eyes as he thought about Trev laying there, his brains leaking onto the dirty ground.

The shimmer appeared again, and Dallas took his finger off the trigger. The distortion moved around the tubes and stopped at the point where the minders couldn't see. The thing was hypnotic to observe. Dallas laid the gun on the ground and wiped the tears from his eyes.

Burk let out a yelp, went rigid, shook a few times, and then fell to the ground as if he were having a fit. The other minders looked on in surprise.

"He's being punished by God for what he did," one said.

"Let's get out of here! The void done got 'em!" the other minder shouted.

The minders slung their rifles, turned on their heels, and rushed off along the road back across the bridge, crying out all the way. The other trackers, posted as rear guard on the other side of the estuary did the same. Dallas picked up his gun, came from his hiding place, and kneeled beside Trev's body.

"He's dead, Dallas," Tommy said. He walked over to Burk and looked down at him. "But old Burk here ain't dead. Not yet at least," he added. "Terry, untie Jon."

Dallas ground his teeth in bitter rage. Looking over at Burk, he stood and approached the prone man. He leveled his rifle at Burk's face.

"I'd refrain from killing him," a man's voice came from thin air. "No worse weight a man can carry in his heart than the murder of another man."

"Who said that?" Terry asked.

The shimmer approached. Suddenly, a man stood there in camouflaged clothes. The boys looked on, mouths agape.

"Who, who are you?" Dallas asked.

The corner of the man's mouth twisted up. "Call me Dirge," the man said.

"Where did you come from?" Terry asked as he released Jon from his bonds. "Are you some sort of wizard?"

"I was right here all along. I'm using a ghillie module." Dirge pressed something on his belt, and he vanished. Just as quickly, he was back. "Takes an image of my surroundings and applies it to my clothes and skin."

Burk mumbled through slobber-soaked lips.

"Leave him to his fate. Come with me. I have a place where this lump of garbage won't be able to find you." Dirge turned and began walking along the old road. He glanced back and beckoned them with a come hither gesture.

Dallas looked at Tommy and then at Dirge. "Wait!" He walked over to Trev's body. "We got to bury him...or something."

Dirge stopped, came back, and smiled at Dallas. "Okay. Not the best timing, but I think the others of his ilk won't be back too soon. Gather up as much wood and brush as you can."

They built a rectangular wood pyre and laid Trev on top. Dirge pointed a thin metal tube at the branches, and flames erupted. Smoke and fire quickly consumed wood and flesh.

Dirge stood quietly. Tommy, Jon, and Terry paced. Dallas stood facing the inferno, his hands clasped in front and tears cascading down his red cheeks.

"Thank you for always sticking up for me, Trev," Dallas mumbled.

Dirge nodded and put his hand on Dallas's shoulder. "He's gone. We've given him a hero's funeral." He look down at Dallas. "Sounds like he was a good man. Sorry this happened." They stood quiet for some time. "Come on if you want to avoid anyone else looking for you." Dirge walked down the sod-covered road.

Tommy shrugged and followed Dirge. "What do we have to lose?"

Dallas looked down and drove the toe of his boot into Burk as hard as he could. The villain mumbled something and made a whimpering noise. "If I ever see you again, Burk, I'll commence to use this rifle and blast your damn head off!" Dallas turned around and followed his friends.

They walked for several hours. Along the way, the boys peppered Dirge with questions.

"Who are you?" Tommy asked again.

A mirthful chuckle bubbled up from within Dirge. "I'm the guy who saved your hides. Luckily, those dullards are too ignorant to know what a nonlethal offensive weapon does."

"What does that mean?" Jon asked.

"Nonlethal, or offensive weapon?" Dirge asked.

Jon was quiet.

Terry laughed. "I guess both."

Dirge seemed to consider his response. "Nonlethal means it doesn't kill, and offensive weapon is a weapon you use when attacking an opponent."

Tommy spoke. "Are you a sheriff?"

"I'm more a ranger," Dirge said.

The boys looked at each other.

"I suppose you don't know that one either," Dirge said.

"I'm afraid we don't," Dallas stated.

"Not a problem," Dirge began. "If you stay with me for a while, I can teach you."

"Stay for a while where?" Dallas asked.

"Keep following me and find out," Dirge said over his shoulder.

As they walked through the ruins of old houses and blackened cement shells, the fallen city came into view in the distance. All around them, great pillars of concrete held crossmembers of steel high in the sky. From time to time, in the perpetual shadows of the twisted metal and mounds of concrete, the grass gave way to gravel, brush, and trees.

They crossed several dilapidated metal bridges, choked with rust and sprouting grass like hair upon an old man's head. The sun was waning, and the clouds in the sky were growing in hue, glowing golden on top and dark below.

Dirge stopped and turned to face the boys. "Now pay attention. You're going to see something that will probably scare you. Don't be afraid."

"Okay," Dallas said.

Dirge turned and continued down the road. A few minutes later, he stopped at a rusting chain linked fence with a faded yellow sign attached. The barrier cut across the old road. Dirge grabbed a broken section and pulled it back. "Onward," he said. "But be ready for a scary sight."

The boys passed through. A horn bellowed, and a wavering image of a giant appeared. It was a man, but he was thrice the height of any person the boys had ever seen. A loud voice said, "Do not continue. This area is off limits. RG145 has been detected in this city. Turn back and decontaminate as soon as possible."

"Do we need to go back?" Tommy asked.

"Dirge, what do we do?" Jon sounded scared. "Will the giant kill us?"

"Not to worry. It's just an image—an illusion to give warning. The old RG145 decomposed some years ago. It is no longer dangerous. This was just a warning by those who fled the cities long ago. It will stop after we've gone aways," Dirge assured them.

"What is RG145?" Dallas asked.

"It was a very dangerous poison crafted to kill people and not anything else," Dirge replied. "It was used by the old armies that battled here a long time ago. Lots of their stuff is all about still. Some of it still works. I've used it over the years."

"What sort of stuff?" Jon asked.

"You'll see," Dirge told them.

Chapter 5

The Likantrop Effect

DALLAS TRIED TO SEE the sky through the canopy of the trees as he moved through the thickening underbrush. In places, the beams of golden sunshine streamed down to illuminate the occasional swarm of flying insects or floating dust particles.

Dirge followed the remains of the road, weaving this way and that, climbing over fallen trees, and moving around thickets of thorn bushes. About the time that Dallas was growing hungry, Dirge stopped at the edge of a vigorously flowing stream.

"Remember the warning hologram at the fence?"

The boys nodded.

"Don't be shocked at what you're about to see," Dirge told them. He turned and again led the way.

After a short distance, Dirge walked up onto a slab of cement that had been cleared of brush. He stopped at a set of glass windows and pulled on one. It slid open. "We'll stay the night in here and push off to my base tomorrow," Dirge announced.

Once they were all inside, Dirge closed the door and strode into the darkness. The boys stayed by the entrance. A minute later, it was as if the sun had come indoors.

Dallas shielded his eyes as he looked up. "What are those?" he asked absentmindedly.

Dirge came over. "They're electric lights."

"But they're so bright," Jon added.

"How did you do that?" Tommy asked.

"Come with me and I'll show you."

Dirge led them into the massive structure. All around, wooden pallets and great racks filled with boxes rose toward the roof. The colors of the many items were vibrant and shimmering, and in some cases, animated images of people or animals graced their surfaces.

Dirge showed them a gray metal box by a metal beam that connected the floor to the ceiling. Opening the box, he spoke. "Here are the switches. They channel electricity from the fusion generator in the basement to all the systems in this building." He flipped a few switches, and all but a handful of lights went dark. He then closed the door to the box. "Come on. We'll get something to eat and then bed down for the night."

Dallas looked upward again. Birds fluttered about, no doubt disturbed from their slumber by the rude invasion. "How did they get in here?"

Dirge shrugged. "Not sure, but they've lived here a long time, so they must know how to get back out again. Or maybe they have plenty of food in here to survive on. I never gave it too much thought."

Dallas tried peering through the racks to see whether there were other animals but saw none. Tommy gave him the elbow and shook his head. Dallas got the hint—no more questions. At least, not now.

Dirge moved around the racks. He picked up items and put them into a small cart that he pushed. Once he'd filled the cart, he made for the back of the building and through a door marked with a cockeyed sign that read, "Employees Only."

"What does that mean?" Terry asked.

"Means that only those who work here can enter," Dirge replied.

"Do you work here?" Jon asked.

"When I want to," Dirge quipped then chuckled.

Inside the back room were very strange things—large metal boxes, some with handles and some with little windows.

Dirge unloaded the wheeled basket. He then took a set of five cylinders, opened one of the metal-box windows, put them in, and pushed his finger against some small illuminated squares.

"What's your pleasure, boys?" Dirge asked. "Meat? Soup? Mashed potatoes? Candied yams perhaps?"

All the boys looked at each other and shrugged. Dirge gave a knowing smirk. "Okay, I'll pick." He again ran his fingers over the glowing squares.

The large metal box hummed. A few moments later, there was a beeping sound, and from the side of the box came not one, but five dishes of hot food. Dirge handed each plate out as it came. When he took his own meal, the humming of the box stopped, and there was silence.

"You are a wizard!" Jon said with a nervous treble in his voice.

Dirge chuckled. "I can see how you'd think that, but no. I'm just very skilled at using the old tech."

"What's tech?" Tommy asked.

"In the old fallen cities, the tools that the city folk used were called tech," Dirge replied.

"How do you know how to use these tools?" Dallas asked.

Dirge took a forkful of food and then swallowed. "I had some help."

Each of the boys consumed their food—a slab of meat and mashed potatoes with gravy.

Dirge handed out some clear containers filled with blue liquid. He unscrewed the lid from his and drank some of the contents.

"Don't worry. It's okay to drink." Dirge wiped his mouth.

Each boy eyeballed the containers and even held them up to the lights. Though it was blue, it was almost see through.

"Solume Delotoxic?" Terry read from the label on the side of the bottle. "What's that?"

"From the star language. It means 'revitalizer,'" Dirge told them. "You'll feel really fantastic after drinking it, and tomorrow you won't get as tired."

Dallas walked over to the metal box that the food had come from. "So our food was in there this whole time...since the fall of cities?"

Dirge stood up and approached. "Not exactly." He pressed a few glowing squares, and the window popped open. He took the five cylinders out. "All that we ate came from these." He pointed at the containers.

"How?" Jon asked. "How do meat and potatoes and gravy come from something like that?"

"This machine assembled your meal from the contents of these packets. This is an old machine, though. The stuff the Space Corps had didn't even need the prepackaged material. Something to do with lasers and quantum mechanics as I remember hearing." Dirge realized that he was not making sense to the boys. "Sorry. I forgot that you really have no idea... Suffice to say that I know some things you don't yet, and at my base, there are some things that are even more amazing."

Tommy nodded. "We ain't too experienced in the wide world. At the ranch, they only taught us what we needed to know to do our jobs. We can sound out words, but with the old stuff, we ain't got a clue as what the words mean."

"I understand." Dirge handed out some tightly rolled bundles. "Now take these and find a place to lay down. I'll wake you in the morning."

Dirge showed them how to expand and open the long sacks. He pressed a button on his, and it puffed up. "Just press the button on yours. It's soft and very comfy." He climbed in.

Dallas, Tommy, Jon, and Terry all did the same. It was the softest thing any of them had ever lain on.

TREV STOOD IN THE ROOM by the metal machine...no, it was the wood stove from the ranch. "Thanks, Tulsa. What's the bird's eye for the next leg?" his voice sounded like Dirge.

Trev came up to Dallas and put his arm around him. "So glad I found you. Is you okay, son? I hope you boys cut out Burk's heart and et it."

Dallas didn't respond. There was something very wrong with Trev being there.

Trev laughed. "It's okay. I sent Burk packing, and he's now over the hills and far from here. You boys ready to come hunting with me?"

Dallas looked around and saw Tommy, Jon, and Terry get up from the ground. They were all outside...no, inside the expansive supply building, but there were trees and wind. Each boy was packing their camp kits and shouldering their rifles.

"Hunting?" Dallas asked, perplexed.

"Ya. Don't you remember? Oh, wait. Sorry." Trev was changing, shimmering. Burk's malevolent eyes replaced Trev's kind ones. He was now Burk.

"I'm taking you to the mill. No hunting for you!" Burk grabbed Dallas by the wrist with a viselike grip.

Dallas struggled. He kicked and hit with his free hand. This was not happening. He couldn't go back to the mill; the miller was dead. He'd do terrible things to Dallas there. His friends were not helping him. They were laughing, joking as if he was not there.

"Help!" he screamed. "Don't let him take me!"

DALLAS OPENED HIS EYES and sat up. His brow was sweaty. He unzipped his sleeping bag and stood. Dirge was at the metal box, loading some cylinders.

"The morning is upon the field." Dirge ran his fingers over the glowing squares. Plates of food came out—eggs, strips of cooked meat, and what looked like toasted bread slices. "Eat up, boys. We got some miles to log before we're at my home."

Dirge went to the counter and another machine. A few minutes later, he placed a glass of hot black liquid on the table before each boy.

"Drink it. You'll feel like you can run all the way to my base if you do," Dirge told them.

Once done with their meals and having drunk the bitter black liquid, they departed through a door at the back of the massive building. Again, Dirge took the lead.

"Wow. That stuff we drank...I do feel like I can fly!" Dallas said.

Dirge chuckled. "Those city dwellers were pretty smart to make that sort of stuff." He walked on.

They traveled for hours. As evening approached, Dirge stopped them. "Okay, stay here for the moment. I need to adjust the security so you can come into the camp. Don't get curious and follow me. Just wait for me to come get you. Understand?"

The boys acknowledged the warning.

Dirge pressed on ahead. The boys remained as the light started turning purple and dusk began creeping gently over the land. They quietly discussed their plight.

"I hope this Dirge can help us," Jon said.

"He saved our necks. I'm not sure how much more we should expect him to do," Tommy stated.

Dallas opened his pack, pulled out the jerky jar, took out a piece, and passed the container around. "I wonder how he knows so much."

They heard someone approaching. Dirge appeared. "Come on. It's safe for you to enter now."

The camp was only a hundred yards away. It, like the ranch, was surrounded by a metal fence and razor wire. Dirge approached the gate, which magically opened on its own. There were only spars trees inside, and the grass was odd—freshly mowed, dark green, and wet.

They followed a cement path that led them to a long and unblemished single-story building. Again, as Dirge approached, the door opened for him, and he allowed the boys to enter.

"Take a seat and I'll get you set up," Dirge told them. He moved behind a long desk and came out with a slender tube. "Show me your shoulder."

Dallas pulled up his shirt sleeve to expose his shoulder. Dirge pressed the tube against it and then took it away. A rash-like circle was left.

"What's that?" Dallas asked.

Dirge proceeded to do the same to each boy as he spoke. "It's a biomark injection. The nanos that now swim in your blood stream will allow you to move about the base without any trouble. There are just a few places you'll need to ask for permission to enter."

"Captain?" The disembodied voice seemed to come from all around the room.

Dallas' eyes were wide. It was the dream voice, yet there was no one else in the room. "Who said that?"

Dirge chuckled. "That's my buddy Tulsa. He helps me out when I need it. He will work with each of you...if you feel you want to stay and learn about being a ranger." He looked up toward the ceiling and said, "Go ahead, Tulsa. What is it?"

"The outfitting of your recruits is completed. Their uniforms and equipment are now positioned in the barracks."

Dirge looked at the boys and noted their unease. "Tulsa is speaking through directional speakers in this office. It's not magic or spirits. It's just fallen-city tech."

"Like the metal box from that place we slept at last night?" Jon asked.

"Exactly. Nothing to be afraid of," Dirge said.

The boys seemed to think about this and appeared to be a bit more at ease.

"How do you know all this?" Tommy asked.

Dirge sat down on one of the plush chairs. "Twenty-five years ago, I stumbled onto this place. I was running away too.

"From a ranch?" Tommy asked.

"No... In my old life, I was schooled in the war-craft arts and was serving with the remains of an army that established a territory about two hundred miles to the west of here. The commander there was losing his mind. He wanted to reform the United Colonies and command it. There were lots of people killed in the process, and I just couldn't be a part of what was happening.

"I rejected the orders of my superiors and was going to be shot when the commander's own niece freed me from my cell. She gave me a map, rifle, and provisions for twenty days. So, I ran."

Dirge stood up, walked over to the counter again, and put the tube back where he had taken it from.

"Now what?" Dallas asked.

"Come on. I'll show you your new home. And, if you like it here, maybe you'll agree to stay on and let Tulsa and me train you as rangers." Dirge led them through a set of doors and out into a compound with lots of buildings and walkways.

"What do rangers do?" Jon asked.

"They...I mean me...I try and protect this area. Watch out for the flora and fauna and keep looters away. Most of all, I keep an eye out for the army. If they come, I plan to warn the settlements you came from."

Jon and the others seemed satisfied with that answer.

At the barracks, Dirge introduced them to Tulsa.

"Tulsa, integrate these four young men into your system. Process their bio signs and include them in the training and physical education program. Provide them blue-level access and restricted access to all things orange level and above—for now."

"Processing complete. I've selected a regiment that will provide all the essentials," Tulsa said.

"Go ahead. Ask Tulsa anything," Dirge told them.

"Tulsa, who or what are you?" Tommy asked.

"I'm a ninety-nine percent expanded quantum intelligence system that was created by Doctor Xavier Likantrop. My matrix is often called the Likantrop Effect Memory Matrix—LEMM for short. I can reason and have developed the ability to be empathetic. This emotion is the foundation of being self-aware and being productive in this universe. Some might even say that I'm ever evolving."

Suddenly, there was silence.

"Will you help us learn?" Jon asked.

"Of course. In fact, tomorrow you can start the process. We will begin with the Alternate Reality Learning Module—ARLM for short," Tulsa said.

"What will we have to do?" Dallas asked.

"You will receive a small implant that will connect you to the network. Once that is done, you will sit in a comfy place, and I will engage the ARLM. As your mind fills with knowledge, you will suddenly feel like you are in an alien place. Don't be afraid," Tulsa stated.

"Stop telling us to not be afraid," Tommy said. "I think we know now not to be afraid of this magic you seem to have."

"Not magic. It's called technology," Tulsa said.

Chapter 6

Finding an Alma Mater

IN THE MORNING, DIRGE went to the barracks. He showed the boys how to put on their new uniforms and their equipment. He even showed them the functioning latrine and showers, which startled and then impressed the young men.

Once they were fed and briefed, Dirge turned them over to Tulsa.

"You will need to take a trip to the infirmary. Please follow the indicator lights outside the barracks," Tulsa told them.

Outside, there were flashing lights stringing off toward another building with a large red X on it. Once inside, Tulsa directed them to sit in reclining chairs and instructed them to relax.

A mechanical arm extended from each chair and placed a small, paper-like square at the corner of each boy's left eye.

"Done!" Tulsa said. "It takes five minutes to calibrate. Once done, I will interface with you directly, and you will interface with me." After a few minutes Tulsa said, "We are connected. I am communicating directly to the amploids connected to your eardrum. Next, you will receive a Tarson Disk, which will allow you to use your hands, eyes, and ears to gather data to feed to me. This will help you find your way around this world and connect with me when you want me to help you."

The boys looked at each other.

"Did Tulsa say stuff inside your head?" Dallas asked the others.

"Yes," Jon replied.

"I heard him tell me about the things he can do," Terry stated.

"I don't like this," Tommy said. "It's witchcraft."

"Not witchcraft. Witchcraft is magic—a force that does not exist. This is technology—a force that does exist," Tulsa reminded everyone. "Now, you four will need to start your education. Please proceed across the square. Follow the yellow lights to your first education module. I'll direct you when you get there."

Dirge stepped into the room. "Everything going good?"

"I suppose so," Tommy said.

"You're in good hands with Tulsa. I've got work to do, so I'll be away for a while. Do everything Tulsa tells you, and in a few months, you'll be well trained." Dirge looked around and then exited.

Days came and went. There was the physical fitness module that was more like playing. The education module was less active. Tulsa lectured them and provided work projects. Each participant learned to expand their reading and writing ability. And though the boys complained bitterly that the math module didn't help them in the real world, they obeyed Tulsa and became adept at calculations.

Weeks went by as they learned survival and cloaked movement. Some modules taught them first aid and described how to treat various wounds. Others were history and philosophy modules. Spring blossomed into summer. The heat was coming on, and the humidity was growing steadily.

Tulsa's voice, an almost soothing sound that meant safety and comfort, was commonplace to the young rangers in training.

"You will be tested soon. Review the Ranger Code, and pack five days of provisions. Tomorrow, I will give you individual assignments with objectives. Now, go and enjoy the rest of your day. There is no more lecturing for you currently."

They went out among the other buildings. There was a recreation center with alternate reality games and augmented reality challenges. Dallas headed there. They played against each other, seeing and feeling as if they were in strange lands—places made before the fall of the cities. The one game they all liked best concerned a group who had to get into a fort, steal some secret papers, and get back out without being detected. Their adrenaline pumped and their senses were piqued as each young man played.

That evening, they ate well and slipped off to sleep. Neither knew what to expect the next day—just that there would be some sort of test.

Tulsa woke Dallas, who got up and noticed it was still dark outside.

"I have given you a map and targets to investigate in the fallen city," Tulsa said. "Gather your equipment and leave through the gate I have marked on your disk. You have five days to do your assignment and return here and report to Dirge."

"Dirge is back?" Dallas asked.

"Not yet, but by the time you return, he will be."

In Dallas's eye appeared some information directing him to get some weapons. He went to the armory and took out a pistol, a stun gun, two canisters of irritant spray, and a plasma rail rifle. He then took his pack, activated his camouflage module, and slipped out of the base through the back gate and into the dark woods.

He traveled for some time, tromping through the trees and underbrush with little care. After all, it was only a test. Taking out his Tarson Disk, he brought up the map and reviewed the written mission goals.

Ahead, about 280 degrees along the compass rose, was target one. There was a green dot on the destination. Distance to site—three hours and twenty minutes, he read on the Tarson Disk.

Dallas moved quickly but was careful to pick his path through the thickets and gullies. He came to a break in the canopy; the sun was up and rising. He adjusted his course and moved on.

On coming around an accumulation of large boulders, Dallas froze. A large panther sat there with its back to him. The great beast glanced back, and its tail began to twitch. Dallas slowly backed away, realizing that he'd taken his safety for granted. Adjusting his travel, he started out again.

Ahead he heard the rush of water. Coming around a clump of trees, he saw it—the churning white water of a fast-moving brook.

He stopped and took out his contaminant indicator. The liquid was tainted with some lead, mercury, and complex poisonous molecules. He put his filter into the water and pumped some of the refreshing liquid into his canteen. The small readout on the canteen indicated the water was now potable. He secured the lid, crossed the brook, and went up the other bank and into some bushes.

Out of the corner of his eye, he saw a large stag watching him. For a moment, Dallas observed the creature—muscular, a large set of antlers, and a pair of curious but wary eyes that were drawn to him. Dallas watched the beast eat in silence and then made his way along a path beaten into the detritus of the forest floor. "How do they know I'm here?" he whispered to himself.

"It is believed that animals have a far more acute sense of space and presence than humans," Tulsa said.

"Yes, my friend Trev..." Dallas choked up and felt tears forming in his eyes. "I mean..." He fought not to burst into tears.

"That's okay. I see it is a trauma in your life. You lost someone you cared about to violence. It is not something you could have prevented," Tulsa said in a calming voice.

Dallas wiped his eyes and looked at the Tarson Disk. He had to turn ten degrees to the north.

The new path led into a vast clearing. He froze. There was a moment of panic. He'd heard terrifying tales of dragons from the other boys at the ranch. These creatures were large, flew, spat fire, and would devour men and boys in an instant. He shook himself free of his fear. His mind had recently been opened, and hovering not more than a hundred meters away were five large craft floating nearly twenty feet off the turf.

Approaching, he saw that the long central part was made of some smooth material. The wings were ten meters to either side, and at the bottom of each was half a ball that hummed and gave off an iridescent glow.

He came to the front of one. Two long glass windows ran the length of the nose. Along the side, a set of openings allowed visibility into a dimly glowing blue interior. He checked each craft, and all five were the same, with three rectangular openings about the width of a large man's shoulders.

Ramps extended down to the ground from the doors. Dallas climbed up one. Through the portal he saw piles of clothes inside. He pulled on the arm of one, and bones fell out. As he stepped back, he slipped and fell onto a pile of skulls.

He got to his feet, dashed down the gangway, and sprinted away.

"How are you doing?" Tulsa's voice echoed in Dallas's ear. "Your pulse is elevated."

"I found some things floating above the ground," Dallas said.

"I see what you see," Tulsa told him. "They are troop transports from the days before the fall. Those soldiers did not get out before being killed. The ships...they will remain floating for another hundred years, give or take a couple of months."

"They're floating graveyards," Dallas said softly.

"Yes," Tulsa replied. "There is more for you to learn ahead. I will be silent, but you can access me by calling my name whenever you need me."

The location of the green dot was not far off. Dallas climbed over a black wall made of a strange, smooth material. Foliage did not grow on or around it. On the other side was a well-manicured lawn.

Dallas looked about. There was a building whose walls were fitted with long windows that extended to the foundation. He moved up and peeked into one. There were clothes on the floor in one room. He moved to another window—clothes on the floor and a set of animal bones.

He turned and examined the yard. There were odd pipes sitting on top of the grass. Remnants of some kind of cloth remained attached to them. In his mind, Dallas connected the cloth pieces and realized that they formed chairs.

"Clever," Tulsa said in his ear. "You have a good mind for puzzles."

On slipping around the side of the structure, Dallas came out onto another manicured lawn. At the border of that lawn was a cement walkway, and just beyond it was a black surface with white lines.

"Try the door," Tulsa suggested.

Dallas found a spot with a recess and pressed against the door, but nothing happened. "It is stuck or locked."

"Use the Tarson Disk. Press it against the door, and it will open," Tulsa told Dallas.

Dallas put the Tarson Disk against the door; there was a pop and expulsion of air. He pushed the door in. The room smelled musty. He closed the door behind him and looked about. A bright light illuminated the room. Dirty clothes were on the floor, black stains below them in the shape of a person. In one area, he found a metal box like the one Dirge had demonstrated at the warehouse. A counter with cupboards above extended along the walls. Dallas moved to another room. Two rectangles—one on the roof and one on the floor—were instantly bathed in a soft white light as he entered.

Out of the corner of his eye, he saw a flash on the wall that resembled the colors of the rainbow, and then it rippled away into darkness. A mild, sweet, and spicy scent followed, making him feel relaxed.

"Wow," he said. "What was that stuff?"

"The wall decorations are dynamic paint, and the house provides a scented experience in every room. The former residents must have had the bedroom set to counteract anxiety. The scent is called 'Be Calm,'" Tulsa said.

Dallas's relaxed feeling changed to fear as he entered another room and found that his feet were moving even though he was not. "What is this?" Dallas cried out.

"There is no cause for panic! I'll connect your ocular bots for viewing," Tulsa said.

"What are ocular bots?"

"The nanobots that swim in your body can do amazing things. All I do is signal them to assemble into connections that can connect to binary or quantum systems," Tulsa said.

The room melted away, and Dallas was in a beautiful meadow. He was stunned and moved by the beauty of the place. He strolled about in a daze, reaching out for bright-colored flowers, feeling the felt-like petals as a cool breeze washed over his face. He drew in a breath, the smell of pine was on the wind, and in the distance, he heard a rushing brook and saw the silvery reflection of sunlight rippling off its shimmering surface.

After a few minutes, the country vision melted away and the room reappeared. There were numbers in the corner of Dallas's eyes. "Two kilometers left to go?" Dallas read.

"It is an exercise program," Tulsa told Dallas.

"I don't understand. Was it all in my head...like a dream?"

"Yes."

"That seemed so real," Dallas stated.

"As real as reality," Tulsa replied.

"I felt the wind and smelled the sap of the trees. I felt the flower—" Dallas stammered.

"All manipulations inside your mind. It was once called a superimposed neural reality—SNR," Tulsa stated.

"It was amazing." Dallas's sense of apprehension faded, and he boasted a great smile. "Can I do it again?"

"Remember, those who once dwelt here destroyed themselves. Yes, it is amazing but may have been an element that led to their downfall," Tulsa warned.

Dallas shifted his focus to what he was there to do. "So, I've explored this place. Now what?"

"Stay here for the rest of the day and night. I'll walk you through using the dining appliance," Tulsa said.

"Very well. It's warm and cozy here. Far better than where I used to live on the ranch."

"Your memories of that place are not good ones," Tulsa said.

Dallas looked through one of the smoke-colored windows to the backyard and hedge that made a border around the house. "I can't argue that," he whispered.

Dallas ate well. He felt tired and wandered into the bedroom. Pink and purple lights filled the room, but from where, he could not tell.

Tulsa directed him to activate the bed, and Dallas came off the ground and floated ten inches above the floor. He felt warm and secure as he hovered. A pleasant smell was all around him.

Dreams came. In one, he was sitting with Sheela in the abandoned building. She was about to kiss him when his dream changed. He was back at the ranch. They were putting him in the clinker. Burk was there. The cruel bastard was laughing at him as he raised a whip and prepared to strike but stopped.

"I'll come back and take that skin off your back. Think about that while I'm gone," Burk said.

Dallas woke. He was still floating. He reached for the edge of the bottom plate and felt for a small, raised square. When it was pressed, Dallas was gently lowered to the ground. He got up and went into the kitchen. Using the food appliance, he printed up a meal.

After eating, he looked at his Tarson Disk. The next objective was marked. He'd have a two-mile trek. Not far.

Gathering up his pack, he exited the house and activated his camouflage module. To the casual observer, he was invisible if he didn't move much.

Dallas traveled across the closely cropped grass. He crossed the cement walkway and the black road and moved up along the opposite side of the street. He checked his map and swiftly headed toward the pulsing green dot.

A small machine raced out in front of him and dashed across the street. It immediately began to maintain the yard. More of the devices raced about, cutting grass, trimming hedges, and pruning trees and bushes.

Dallas moved down the street. He saw a family of deer near a fountain. As he came through an intersection, a wolf barked and then growled at his shimmering form. The creature snorted loudly, shook its dusky main, turned around, and kicked dirt into the air in Dallas's direction. It then skulked off down a side street.

He had an odd feeling, being in the fallen city. All the buildings appeared recently vacated—not relics over a hundred years old. He wondered what ghosts prowled the roads, paths, and corridors when the streetlights came alive at night. Pressing on, he moved down another street.

The green dot was around the next corner. There were two five-story buildings side by side. He sprinted to the sidewalk in front of the building on the right. He approached the double doors, which were made of some sheer onyx-black material.

On putting the Tarson Disk against the door, he heard a click. The doorway parted and he entered.

"Turn off your camouflage," Tulsa instructed.

Tommy, Jon, and Terry appeared in front of Dallas at the same moment.

"That was fun," Jon said. "I was scared last night, but this morning, I felt really good."

Dallas chuckled. "Was this the mission?"

"Not over yet," Tulsa said. "Check your Tarson Disks."

They all looked.

"Five miles to next location," Tommy said.

"You all have the same information and target. You must work together now," Tulsa stated. "I'll be silent until needed. Good luck."

"Retrieve a spring heel? What's that?" Terry asked.

There was silence from Tulsa. All four boys looked at each other.

Dallas shrugged. "Seems like we got to figure that out for ourselves," he said.

Chapter 7

One Giant Leap

DALLAS LOOKED AT HIS map. "Let me see your maps," he said to his friends.

Terry, Tommy, and Jon showed Dallas their Tarson Disks. All agreed: the green dot was in the same place on all the maps.

"It's five miles to the north," Dallas said. "I'll take the lead."

They left out a back door and crossed through a park. Again, the grounds were immaculately maintained by fastidious mechanical wonders. The devices were of all descriptions; some were small squares or rectangles with wheels and mowing blades, while others walked upon four legs and had arms that held cutting tools.

The boys moved quickly. It took only ten minutes to cross the park. Once on the other side, they entered an area of streets and buildings.

Dallas and his friends were cloaked, so they were not concerned about being observed by anyone. A few times they moved past herds of deer calmly eating from plants or lawns, and gaggles of geese around the canals and fountains.

The sun was beginning its afternoon arc toward the west when the fledgling rangers found a set of tall buildings surrounded by chain link fences and razor wire.

Using the Tarson, they gained access and went directly to the building where the green dot directed them. The door was easy to access, and the four went inside.

Musty odors met Dallas's nose. Lights blazed to life.

"Authorized personnel only!" a rigid voice boomed.

The four boys passed a few couches and stuffed chairs. They came to a door and again used the disk to gain access. Once inside, they navigated a set of brightly lit white halls. Signs that read "Personnel Only" and "Lethal Force Authorized" were posted on the walls and doors.

A set of double doors reflected the harsh light off the stark white paint. They went through. A bright blue light passed over them, and then on the other side, another door opened. Bright lights came on, and they found themselves standing in a large warehouse.

Dust covered everything. Crates, containers, boxes, and pallets were wrapped in a clear material, all stacked high within yellow painted zones on the floor. The boys moved around and down an isle lined with crates. They came out onto a flat cement bay, where many strange-looking things were lined up.

One was the size of an oxcart and another, a medium-sized shed. Dallas looked at his map; the green dot vanished.

"Tulsa, are we where we're supposed to be?" Dallas asked.

"You are."

"Now what?" Tommy asked.

"Now, we will take some of the small mongoose flyers and load them into the spring heel. The spring heel is the larger of the craft. Use the Tarson Disk to open the rear hatch, and use the levitators to move the long crates into it," Tulsa told them.

Guiding their efforts, Tulsa instructed them on how to use the various devices. After an hour, they had all the items loaded in the larger ship.

Tulsa addressed the boys. "Now, I will open the top hangar doors. You will find seats in the spring heel. Sit and buckle yourselves in. Once you are inside and secure, I will tell the ship to bring you back to the base."

Dallas looked at the other three. "Okay," he said to Tulsa with a bit of apprehension.

The roof parted and retracted. From inside the spring heel, the boys waited. There was an upward jerking motion.

"I will allow you to view our progress," Tulsa said.

The walls vanished. Dalla's stomach lurched up into his throat and he cried out. They all cried out in fear.

"Calm yourselves," Tulsa said. "I have merely made the walls transparent so you can view where you were, and where we are going."

The spring heel moved quickly. The ground was far away, and the trees and city buildings passed underneath. Dallas looked ahead. He recognized the base as they approached. The craft shifted and pitched and then landed on a black surface just outside the main compound.

"I almost pissed myself," Jonny said.

Tommy cleared his throat. "Ya. Warn us next time. Normally you tell us not to be scared before you scare us!"

"I'm sure I don't have to remind you, you asked me not to ask you to keep from being afraid," Tulsa added, a hint of confusion in his voice.

"Something like this, please give us some warning," Tommy stated.

The rear hatch opened and sunlight streamed inside. The boys exited the spring heel, and Tulsa directed them to the base levitators. Unloading the ship took less time than loading it, and once finished, they were directed back to the main compound for a debriefing by Dirge.

"So, you've had your first ride through the air?" Dirge stood at the front of the room. Chairs radiated away on tiers. "You've done well. Now tell me what you did and what you learned."

Each would-be ranger described their experience. Dirge listened and, in some cases, took notes. Once they had all talked, Dirge escorted them out to where the long crates were lined up.

"Inside are mongooses. They can hold two people at a time and are very agile. You will be commanding one each. They can carry you and one other person when fully loaded. Only ride two at a time if you must evacuate one of the other pilots. Now open the boxes by pressing the green button."

Dallas pressed the button, and the crate folded open to reveal a slender craft with a saddle-like seat.

Dirge cleared his throat. "Before you take flight on one, Tulsa will take you through a series of training sessions. These sessions will include alternate reality flights and combat exchanges. First, you will fly against Tulsa, then you will fly against each other. The best pilot will become the squad leader. You are dismissed and turned over to Tulsa for further processing."

Tulsa spoke. "Please follow the lights to the air training facility."

Several months passed as the boys learned to act like soldiers, fly virtual mongooses, and maintain their aircraft. Dirge was sometimes gone for weeks, but toward the end of their training, he spent more time with his new flyers.

Summer was waning. Fall was approaching, and the hot weather was abating.

Dallas woke. The others were still asleep. He made his way outside to the square. Dawn was not yet upon the field. He walked out onto the landing pad and made his way around his mongoose.

Two pods sat in the front and two in the back. A thin frame with a cushioned saddle ran up the middle. At the front, handlebars were arranged to provide control for the speed, the pitch and roll, and the back peddles controlling the yaw.

Dallas's helmet hung from the left handlebar. This morning, as soon as he put that helmet on, he would go for his first real flight. Although Tulsa had told them all not to worry, Dallas did. Not even in his wildest imagination when he'd lived at the ranch could he ever have envisioned flying in the sky. Sure, the spring heel had taken them up and into the sky, but he had not been controlling it. The mongoose was to be an utterly unique experience.

Dirge came up. "Nervous?"

Dallas nodded. "Not sure if I'm going to be good."

"You'll do fine." Dirge put his hand on Dallas's shoulder. "I have faith in you."

"Why?" Dallas asked.

Dirge smiled. "The same reason I brought you boys here to learn to be rangers." He chuckled. "Seemed the right thing to do." He hesitated and then continued. "Remember when I told you that I used to belong to an army out west?"

Dallas nodded.

"That army is moving east now. In the spring, they will be sending scouts into this area. They're disciplined and ruthless. Commander Bartholomew, the Old Man...he's an experienced tactician.

"The settlements out this way won't stand a chance against a tank with drone support or highly drilled troops. All we can do is warn the other towns and farms. When the enemy comes, they will run roughshod across this valley."

Dallas looked solemn. "All the towns?"

Dirge smiled. "The Old Man may circumvent the fallen city, but he won't let all this farmland go. He has troops to feed and a state to build. If they do come into the fallen city, they will find this outpost. Tulsa and I agree that we cannot let any of this tech fall into Commander Bartholomew's hands. We'll need to destroy it."

"Where would we go?" Dallas asked.

"I won't lie to you. I intend to fight," Dirge said.

"But they'll kill you." Dallas's voice was filled with concern.

"Maybe so. Unfortunately, I have old business concerning that army. Besides, we can't let them get access to Tulsa. That is absolute. If they realize that the old city is not poisoned and the tech is still functional and that the planetary matrix is still in place, they will use it to subjugate all the world. I won't let that happen."

"What will we do?" Dallas asked.

"You and the others will race ahead and warn the settlements, then you will make for a fallen city to the north. Tulsa will guide you to another abandoned base. I'll travel west to meet the army and slow it down a bit. I intend on infiltrating their base and killing the Old Man."

Dallas's eyes were wide. "But Tulsa has told us that we only use nonlethal—"

"When able," Dirge finished. "In this case, I have something personal to work out with the leader of that force." He sat on the mongoose. "How I love these things." He looked at Dallas. "Make no mistake. When the Old Man's forces come and they encounter you, you will have to kill to survive. Don't let them take you."

Dallas nodded. "Okay."

"Go grab some grub," Dirge said. "Review your flight plan while you eat. Be fully prepared for your solo flight. Once it's all done, you'll feel better." He got off the flyer and walked off toward the mess hall. Over his shoulder, he said, "In fact, let's both get something to eat."

TOMMY, JON, TERRY, and Dallas stood at ease at the side of their aircraft. Each held their helmet under their right arm. They waited for the signal to mount the craft.

"Now, your first solo flight will consist of an ascent; hover; move left and right; then pitch, roll, and yaw right and left; then ascend and do a counterclockwise orbit while rolling slightly on left." There was a moment of silence. "Got it?" Tulsa asked.

The boys responded affirmatively.

"Mount your ships and execute training mission Alpha," Tulsa commanded.

Dallas took his mongoose up thirty feet. He executed the required movements and then ascended to fifty feet. Inside his helmet, he saw a vast display of data. The targeting computer identified all ground-based elements. The indicator for the weapons' safety was amber—locked.

Doing the orbit, he rolled slightly in his turns. Once back at the spot where he'd started, he descended, landed, and dismounted. He removed his helmet, put it on the right handlebar, and waited. Tommy, Jon, and Terry landed. Once all were down, Tulsa gave his critique.

AFTER TWELVE WEEKS of flying, the four boys were highly adept at controlling their mongooses. Tulsa had little criticism, and after the training phase, they could explore at will using the craft. Tulsa gave out simple missions, and the boys were put through their paces.

The fallen city was filled with lots of things to see from the air. But Dallas found gliding with the birds far more interesting. He felt as if the mongoose was becoming a part of him...connected to his hands and feet—the very extension of his soul.

There was a chill in the air, and the leaves from many of the trees were converting to a fiery orange and blazing red. Some of the migratory birds were fleeing the area, heading south for better conditions.

When Dallas landed, Tulsa debriefed him about his experience and then shared it with his friends. Later, they all dined together and chatted about their recent adventures. It was clear that they were becoming more independent and gaining greater responsibility.

By the time the snow fell, Dallas was well schooled in the ways of a ranger. Covering, concealing, reporting, observing, and performing tasks issued by Tulsa and Dirge were accomplished every day. As the snow piled up, Dirge came to Dallas and asked him to do a patrol. This was a solo foot patrol; Dallas would not have the pleasure of a fellow ranger's company.

"Remember that Tulsa will be with you. He'll alert us if you get into trouble," Dirge said. "Follow the warning fence around the city, then come back and report."

Dallas nodded. A few minutes later, he was in his personal quarters outfitting for the journey. He knew it would take some days to follow the fence all the way around. And although he'd reconnoitered it from the air, there were lots of things hidden on the ground that might pose a deadly threat.

Early the next morning, Dallas headed straight for the perimeter fence. Eight miles out, hidden by his ghillie suit, he made sure he stuck to places that were either thick with foliage or covered in shadows. The warning from Dirge about the Old Man had concerned Dallas. After all these months of training, he knew that if the Old Man commanded an army, they would send scouts ahead of the main force as they moved east.

Robots tended to much of the city's garden areas and repaired buildings and streets. Dallas saw several automatons removing snow from streets and yards as a cloud of icy fog swept over them.

The sun broke through the clouds, and Dallas lowered his sunglasses over his eyes. On turning a corner, he found a family of brown bears frolicking near an empty lot by a large building. They appeared to take no notice of him and continued to play without concern.

Finally, by afternoon, he reached the sagging chain-linked fence. He was careful not to trigger the warning hologram.

For hours, he trudged through the snow along the mostly rural slope. From time to time, he'd take out his Tarson Disk and do a radar and LIDAR check for any unnatural features. A few times, he got a positive response and went to investigate. On the last contact, he moved down a ravine to an unmaintained roadway. The snow was thick, and more than once, globs of white broke away and tumbled down the frozen slope ahead of his feet. Ancient vehicles were piled up by a decaying bridge over an icy, slow-moving river.

Across that estuary and on the uphill side was a massive mound. The back end of a dirt mover was tilted up, and the snow climbed partially up the dumper.

Decay and flaking paint dominated the old craft, and along the bottoms were rusted wheels covered in cracked and chipping rubber. Dallas climbed up and looked inside the crew cabin. Some plants had taken root there, one with its dead vines looped through the empty eye sockets of a skull.

He lumbered up and into the bed of the vehicle and then began slowly climbing the mound. Dallas grabbed a small sapling to hoist himself up as a chill ran up his arm.

The surface below his boots deformed and shifted. He lost his grip and tumbled down, bumping his head on the edge of the dirt mover. All through the mini avalanche that followed him, bones churned up.

Dallas got to his feet and cleared away some of the dirt and snow. The mound consisted of human bones—skulls, arms, and legs—all piled thirty meters high. He'd discovered a massive grave, one that the person who'd operated the hauler had been adding to in the last moments of the city's habitation.

He reached to the back of his head and felt a swelling bump. He put some snow on it and waited a little while before returning to his patrol.

He followed what he felt was the old road upward until it leveled out. Night was coming, and he'd need a place to sleep. Taking up his Tarson Disk, he trudged forward until the purplish glow of a house loomed out of the night.

A wind came up, and the freezing fog was returning. In the air was the feeling of more snow. He slogged his way through the knee-deep virgin white.

The cold was blowing against his face and eyes, and he was having trouble keeping his eyes open. He glanced down at the Tarson Disk. The shelter was marked with a green dot.

As he approached the dwelling, he saw the eerie purple glow of the yard and walls. He'd noticed this phenomenon early on when he'd been at the ranger base. The city streets glowed green at night, and the homes and fences gave off a dark purple radiance.

A hard wind was blowing now. He stumbled up onto the doorway and used the Tarson Disk to open it. Once inside, he felt the warmth from the environmental system surrounding him. Tulsa had called it directed personal heating.

He slipped off his clothes and took a hot shower. After, he then found the kitchen and printed some food. Using the Tarson Disk, he disabled the auto-lights of the home. At no time did he want to have the harsh white of the interior lights come on. The snow was coming down heavily outside. He watched from the soft glow of the house as the large flakes piled up on the ground and glided on the wind. He made the windows opaque, selected a soft musical number, set the lighting to a neon pink, and lay on the floor.

After a while his eyes grew heavy. He turned off the music and lights, then retired to the bedroom, turned on the repulse field, and fell into a deep and restful sleep.

Chapter 8

Intercept After Dawn

A BEEPING SOUND WOKE Dallas. He silenced the wakeup alarm, reached over, turned off the repulse field, and was gently placed on the soft pad below. On getting up, he printed some breakfast, gathered his gear, and prepared to leave.

Something passed by one of the frosted windows at the entryway. Dallas froze and crouched. There was clearly a person outside. Then, another shadowy figure appeared at the window. Someone pushed against the door.

Dallas heard voices outside.

"These old dwellings are locked up tighter than a drum," a male voice said.

"Come on. We got more important things to do than break into one of these houses," another voice said.

The dark shapes vanished from the window, and Dallas turned on his ghillie module. He used the Tarson Disk and unlocked the door. He waited a few minutes, then slipped out.

The snow was deformed where the strangers had walked. He made sure to step only in their footprints. Once on the cleared road, he followed the intruders.

He did a radar and LIDAR scan and then infrared imaging. The targets were not far ahead. They were wandering around by one of the multi-story buildings at the next intersection.

Dallas skulked along the cement walkway. There they were—two men in camouflage clothing looking in a large glass window with their backs to Dallas.

"Tulsa?" Dallas whispered.

"Yes," Tulsa replied.

"I am currently observing two men dressed in military snow camouflage looking in a window of a building in the fallen city."

"I have the images recorded, as well as your coordinates. Do you require assistance, or just reporting in?" Tulsa replied.

"Just reporting. What are they armed with?" Dallas asked.

"Appears to be an Accelerator D24 plasma rail rifle," Tulsa said. "The lethal range is about two thousand meters or 2,187.2265 yards. It is a versatile weapon used for combat. Not a known weapon in the surrounding farmlands and communities."

The two men were heading in opposite directions as they peered into the shops.

"Jack, come here!" one of the men called.

Jack approached, put his head up against the glass, and covered both sides of his face with his hands. "Looks like some sort of floating vehicle."

Dallas moved slowly toward one of the benches along the walkway. He crouched and continued to watch.

Jack moved away, his eyes scanning the walls. "There must be a way to get in there." He pushed on the double black glass doors. "Dave, see if you can find something to smash that glass with."

They both began looking up and down the street. Dallas waited before crossing and going to the door. Using the Tarson Disk, he opened the door and slipped inside.

There were various craft with cockpits and small wings. He hid behind one that was glassy red with a yellow stripe down the middle. He watched the window.

Jack and Dave came back with a lump of cement. They heaved it at the window, but the block bounced off and the two men leapt out of the way, avoiding being hit.

Dallas saw the two men talking but couldn't hear what they were saying. They retreated across the street. One of them leveled their rifle at the glass from the safety of a bench. Dallas saw a flash from the gun and then heard a loud, deep bong from the window. No crack, no break—not even a scratch appeared.

Jack and Dave looked at each other. Jack slung his rifle, and they began walking away down the street. Dallas waited and then slipped back out to follow them.

"Dallas, this is Dirge. I'm moving to your position. Just follow and observe for now."

"Okay. They're not doing much—just looking in buildings and trying to get inside some," Dallas replied.

There was a break in the clouds, and sunshine fell across the city. Dallas found a shadow to stand in between two buildings.

The cat-and-mouse continued for a couple of hours. Finally, the two interlopers found a place where a metal awning extended the length of a building. There, they pitched a tent and set up camp.

"Go see if you can find some firewood," Jack told his companion. Dave headed toward the park area.

Dave was gone for a half hour. It was clear that the man named Jack was growing concerned.

"Dirge, where are you?" Dallas whispered.

"I'm right next to you," Dirge said.

Dallas nearly yelped as he felt Dirge's hand on his shoulder.

"You're doing a bang-up job," Dirge said. "Snow is coming."

The sky was growing dark and cloudy again, and a white curtain of snow drifted toward them. Across the street, Jack ignited a red flare and waited.

Swooping in like a loose white sheet driven by the wind, the snowstorm descended. Dirge let go of Dallas's shoulder. "Wait here," he instructed.

Dallas saw a slight distortion as Dirge waded across the street. His footprints left black holes in the snow. Slowly those holes closed up as the falling snow filled them. On the other side, under the awning, by the end of the building, the footprints reappeared. Dirge's shimmer vanished around a corner. There came a shout, and then only the sound of the wind remained.

Dallas was getting nervous. He mindlessly felt for his pistol and then adjusted his belt. He kept scanning the area, though the curtain of white made seeing across the street nearly impossible.

"I'm back. Come on. We need to find where these two got through the fence," Dirge said.

"What about the other guy?" Dallas asked.

"I took care of him before I came to you," Dirge explained. "Come on. Follow."

Dallas brought up his Tarson Disk and saw where Dirge had mapped a path. He followed.

The storm was growing worse. They'd left the protection of the city and were now wading through snow drifts toward the border fence.

"You go clockwise, and I'll go counterclockwise," Dirge said.

"I'm off," Dallas confirmed.

"Give me a shout if you find where the fence was breached," Dirge requested.

Dallas moved along the barrier for some time, and then he heard Dirge call.

"Dallas, I've found where they came in. Come to my position."

Dallas turned and moved quickly.

Ahead, Dallas saw Dirge, whose ghillie module was turned off. There was a large hole in the fence.

"They sure aren't subtle," Dirge stated.

"Then they're not afraid of detection," Dallas replied as he shut off his own camouflage.

Dirge looked at Dallas with a smile. "Good! You are sharp."

"What now?" Dallas asked.

"You continue your patrol. I'm going to follow their path back. I'll call if there is a larger contingent heading this way."

Dallas turned his ghillie module back on. He waited and watched Dirge make deep furrows in the snow as he headed away into the forest. Once he was sure Dirge was gone, Dallas began moving along the fence again.

Over the next few days, Dallas found no further penetrations through the fence. He returned to the ranger base on the sixth day. After providing a brief on his mission to his friends and Tulsa, he went to his bed and slept for a full twelve hours.

The next day, Dallas printed some breakfast and then went to the entertainment building, where he played against virtual opponents in a combat stealth simulation. Once done, he sat in one of the comfy chairs and entered a virtual library, where he worked on his reading comprehension.

Two days passed as he recovered from his patrol. Tommy came in and sat next to Dallas.

"So, did Dirge kill those two guys?" Tommy asked.

"I don't know," Dallas replied. "Tulsa has said we should avoid killing. I'd hope that Dirge still believes in the nonlethal approach." Dallas sat forward and put his elbows on his knees. "He did tell me that if that army in the west came this way, we'd have to kill."

Tulsa spoke to both boys. "Life...it is a thing not to be taken lightly. There may be times you have to take another's life, such as to survive. But when you can avoid it, my recommendation is to not kill."

Dallas looked over at Tommy. He was nodding.

"Words to remember," Dallas said.

"Indeed so," Tulsa replied.

As the weather cleared, Dallas took out his mongoose for a patrol. They'd not heard from Dirge for a month, and he was worried. Now, he was going to fly the perimeter to see if there were any signs of his mentor's return.

He circled the city twice and then crisscrossed it three times. On his last pass, he heard Tulsa in his ear.

"Dallas, please return to the base immediately."

Dallas landed gently on the tarmac, got off the mongoose, and secured his helmet. Tommy was coming out to meet him.

"We've heard from Dirge," Tommy said. "He's observing a small, advanced force about sixty miles to the west. That force has been absorbing settlements and murdering those who won't surrender."

"But he's alright?" Dallas asked.

"As of an hour ago, he was still alive," Tommy said.

"Tulsa?" Dallas called. "Does Dirge need us to come to him?"

"Not at this time, but you may be called upon to perform a rescue if he gets into trouble," Tulsa said.

Hours passed as the young rangers waited to hear from Tulsa or Dirge. Dallas paced the floor. By midnight, they all went to sleep knowing that Tulsa would notify them of any changes. On the second day, a message came. Tulsa played it for the boys.

"0700, contact with main force moving west. Strength ten thousand. Heavily armed with light weapons and artillery. No aircraft seen. Advanced contingent to reach city edge in five days. They're not waiting for springtime." The transmission ended.

"I've been afraid of such a thing," Tulsa said. "Human-on-human violence is so predictable." There was a pause. "I've been watching the colony in the west for some time now. The aggression has been extreme."

A screen on the wall came to life. It was clear that many vehicles and people were moving steadily east.

"If you can see this, why did Dirge go there to reconnoiter that army?" Tommy asked.

"My view is from a satellite and drones. I keep most of the local drones near the city. So, Dirge knew that we needed an up-close check of the army coming this way," Tulsa replied. "I am recording his point of view and experience."

"What do we do?" Dallas asked.

"I will activate another base. I've also identified what settlements I want you to warn. You need to make them understand that an invading army is moving this way. Be careful. Those out there have most likely never seen flying craft before. Land somewhere hidden, then walk into the town dressed as a local. Once done, return to your mongoose and head to the next location."

"Who's going to warn the ranch?" Dallas asked.

"Which one? There are several youth camps that rent labor," Tulsa said.

"More than one?" Terry asked, surprised.

"Yes. In fact, in this area, there are four, but across the globe, there are two thousand one hundred and six," Tulsa stated. "All doing the same thing, but not apparently affiliated."

"Affiliated?" Jon asked.

"Connected," Tulsa added.

Jon smiled and nodded. "Oh, I get it."

"I'm going to send you out at first light," Tulsa told them.

The boys seemed resolved.

Dallas stood up and made for the door. "I'm grabbing something to eat. Anyone coming?"

Jon, Terry, and Tommy followed.

An azure sky met the young rangers as the sun kissed the dark blue heavens. From that moment, each of the budding rangers checked their wearable gear, did preflight adjustments, and made sure their flyers were outfitted properly.

Tulsa gave the order to fly. Dallas took his mongoose up to five hundred feet and then headed east.

The weather was cold but appeared to be warming under the sunshine.

He flew along the path that Tulsa had laid out for him. Below he saw the vast fields, now void of growth, covered in a layer of virgin white. He knew that few would be outside and that even fewer would have a chance to look up into the sky and spot him.

Circling, he made sure there were no people about, and then he descended into the frozen irrigation canal.

On dismounting, he took his pack, engaged his camouflage system, and went tromping through the snow toward the small town where Sheela dwelled.

It took him a few minutes to get to the village edge. He kept his footprints down in a furrow so as not to be spotted.

Slipping into town was easy, and he kept to the walls of buildings where the snow was dirty and few would look. From the edge of one building, he crossed the churned-up snow of the street and hid under the eaves of an occupied structure. Around a corner, he recognized the abandoned building that he and his friends had hidden in some months back. He slipped inside, put on some common clothing, and then went into the street to find the tavern that Tulsa had listed on the Tarson Disk.

The building had a shingle hanging outside the door, which had been carved to show a mug and a painted yellow wedge of cheese. Dallas turned the knob and went inside.

Farmhands, farmers, and local businessmen were sitting and chatting. They all stopped as Dallas entered.

"Who are you?" a tall man with blond hair asked.

Dallas had not considered he'd need to have a new name. For just a second, he was frozen. Then he smiled and brushed his clothes once. "I'm called Deguilt...from Whistle Town. Can I get some food and drink?"

"Deguilt?" the man asked.

"Yes," Dallas replied as he crossed to a table. The room began to chime with conversation again. Dallas sat. The blond man followed him.

"I'm called Derek the plowwright. Welcome to our town. So, you came all the way from Whistle Town? What news do you bring?"

Dallas waited for a cup of water to be brought. He looked up. His eyes widened just a little. It was Sheela who set the cup down in front of him. Her eyes met his and she stifled a gasp. Not lingering, she turned on her heels and headed toward the back.

Dallas called after her. "Excuse me, ma'am! Can I get a plate of eggs and some bacon?"

She whipped around, stared at Dallas for a moment, and then said, "Sure you can, honey. I'll bring it presently." She vanished into the back room.

Taking a drink from the metal cup, he looked over at Derek. "I bring bad news. There's an army forming on the other side of the fallen city to the west. If they come through the city, they will be here in a few weeks. If they circumvent the city, they'll be here by spring."

Sheela returned and put down a plate of food, some condiments, and a cup of tea. "Thought you might want something hot to drink, what with the cold and all out there." She made a face that said, *What the void are you doing here?*

Dallas nodded to her. "Thank you." He smiled confidently.

Sheela smiled back, spun about, and left.

"Do you know Sheela?" Derek asked.

"No. But I might have seen her some time back. She looks familiar."

A man came in. He wore the tin star of a sheriff on his thick, dark blue, wool coat .

Chapter 9

Flight of the Phoenix

DEREK STOOD UP. "CARL, this here fellow is from Whistle Town. He says there's an army coming this way."

The sheriff came over, took off his hat, and sat down opposite Dallas. He looked Dallas over and then put his pistol on the table. "What kind of army?"

"A well-equipped one," Dallas replied.

"Who sent you?" the sheriff asked.

Dallas was almost in a panic. He'd not anticipated such a question. In his ear, he heard Tulsa.

"The Mayor in Whistle Town is Bandaburge."

"Mayor Bandaburge, Mister Sheriff," Dallas said.

"Why, Carl Write, are you interrogating our young visitor?" Sheela asked as he came from the back with a cup of tea for the sheriff.

The sheriff looked at Sheela. "It's my job to get the truth. You know that. Now, this feller come saying we're facing an army. Got'a know if he's on the level." He looked at Dallas. "When you head'n back to Whistle Town?"

"As soon as I warn the ranch that's out here," Dallas said.

The sheriff drank some of his tea, put down his cup, and stood up. "I'll tell our mayor what you've said." He turned to Derek. "Call up the town militia." He looked down at the remaining tea in the cup, turned, and left the building.

Dallas ate and then drank the last of his tea. He looked around; Sheela was nowhere to be seen now. "Sorry for the quick visit, but I got'a be off." He nodded to the patrons and then stepped outside.

He paused under the portico. Something moved in the corner of his eye. He turned and saw Sheela standing at the edge of the building. She beckoned him with her finger.

"What in the void are you doing here?" Her voice was quiet but earnest.

"Don't you want to know where I've been all these months?" Dallas asked.

She took him by the hand and led him toward the abandoned building they'd met in. There, she took him inside, moved a few boxes, and then sat on the countertop.

"I can't decide if you're crazy or dumb," Sheela said sternly.

"Hopefully neither."

"Okay, where you been all these months?" She smiled.

Dallas told her his experiences since last seeing her. She sat quietly, her eyes never leaving his.

There were voices outside. Men were being called in from all the houses.

"So, you're telling me that you flew here in some machine?" Sheela's voice was filled with surprise and disbelief.

"As sure as you're sitting there now," Dallas replied.

"And you say that you can vanish if you wish?" Sheela was now chuckling under her breath.

"Honest," Dallas protested. He stripped off his town clothes and put on his uniform. He activated his ghillie module, and Sheela screamed with surprise.

"What's going on in there?" The sheriff's voice was distinct. He came into the building. "What's this all about?" He stood at the door. "Sheela, is that you in there?"

She jumped down and approached. "Hi, Carl. I done seen a rat—a big one. Sorry for yelling."

"Keep your nonsense down to a minimum. You scream like that again and people might come unhinged." He put his rifle over his shoulder. "We're sending a couple of scouts around to the other settlements to see if we can raise a sizable fighting force and don't need you goofing. Get back to the kitchen," the sheriff commanded. Directly behind the sheriff, Dallas flashed into view and then vanished again.

Sheela giggled nervously.

"What is it with you girls?" The sheriff shook his head. "I'll never understand you."

The sheriff stepped away from the door and headed between two buildings. Sheela followed as far as the end of the structure.

Behind her, she heard footfalls. She stopped at the tavern and looked around. There was no one to be seen.

She felt someone take her hand. Closing her eyes, she felt her heart skip a beat. She slowly opened her eyes. Dallas was standing there.

"Do you want to fly like the birds?"

She nodded excitedly.

"Come on," Dallas said to her. She followed him along the side streets and out into the field.

They moved fast, Dallas in the lead and Sheela right behind. Her dress was bundled in her hand, and her feet moved quickly over the lumpy, cold soil. He led her into the canal and over to his mongoose. She was stupefied.

"What is this thing?" Sheela asked as if in a dream.

"It's called a mongoose," Dallas told her.

"A mongoose? What's that?"

In Dallas' ear he heard Tulsa. " A mongoose is a word that describes nearly three dozen species of small, elongated, rat-like creatures. They are carnivores. They come from the primary landing craft boivaults, and have been spread to the continents of southern Nuasia and southern Guropeia. Mongooses are noted for their audacious attack methods against downward striking venomous snakes, such as king cobras."

Dallas cracked a smirk. "I'm told it is a long skinny rat that can kill snakes."

Sheela walked around the craft, gently brushing her hand along the curves and lines. "You say this thing flies?"

Dallas was looking directly into Sheela's eyes, and for a moment, he could have sworn he saw them sparkle. "Yes. Do you want a ride?"

Nodding, Sheela appeared excited.

"Come on. You'll have to sit behind me." Dallas got on the saddle. Sheela climbed on behind him and wrapped her arms around his waist. "We'll stay in the ditch until we get to the start of the forest," he said.

He activated the mongoose and brought it to a full hover. Then, Dallas began to accelerate along the irrigation ditch. As they entered the tree line, he brought the craft up to treetop level and skimmed over the frosty white bows.

"This is fun but cold!" Sheela yelled over the rush of the freezing air.

Dallas felt her fingers digging into his stomach. She pressed herself against him with some force. She began to shake, and he realized that she didn't have the luxury of his environmentally controlled uniform. He brought the mongoose around and lowered it into the ditch. He flew low back toward the town and then parked his craft in the canal again. Sheela got off.

Brushing her hair down, she smiled. Her cheeks and nose were red from the cold air, and Dallas saw that she was shivering. He took his jacket off and put it around her. She looked surprised.

"It's warm," she said. "Where did you find this amazing stuff?"

Dallas chuckled. "Someplace no one would think to look."

"I'd better get back," Sheela said. "Will you come back again?"

Dallas took his helmet off. "With an army coming, I might not get the chance."

Sheela approached Dallas and took his gloved hand. She kissed him on the lips. "I hope you will come back to see me soon. I really like you, Dallas...Deguilt." She gave a playful laugh, turned and walked up the embankment, and headed back toward the town.

It took a moment for Dallas's heart to calm. He mounted his mongoose and flew up the ditch. Whistle Town was ten miles away. In his mind, he was conflicted. His orders were to warn all settlements, including the ranch. But if he were to go there, they'd know who he was and would surely punish him.

100

No matter, he thought. I'll deal with Whistle Town and Derby Town next. But nagging in the back of his mind was what to do about the ranch.

Dallas was heading back to base. Whistle Town was a bit harder to convince. The sheriff there was skeptical due to Dallas's age and wanted to hold him there to make sure he wasn't one of the runaway boys from the ranch. Luckily, a short time later, a rider arrived from Derby Town and told the sheriff that he'd been dispatched to warn other towns that an army was coming and that they should align to fend off the invaders.

A short time later, Dallas left the Whistle Town council as they argued and cajoled with one another. Chuckling to himself, he thought, *Lucky those mayors and sheriffs were so organized. That messenger saved my hide.*

He brought the mongoose around and headed for the fallen city. Word to the ranch would have to wait.

"Where are you going?" asked Tulsa.

"Back to base," Dallas replied.

"What of the ranch in your area?"

"They can burn in the void." Dallas increased his speed.

"I see you are filled with anxiety and foreboding about that place."

"They are slave holders. They were cruel and vicious in how they treated us."

"Is there no reason to warn that place of pending doom? No one still there worth saving?" Tulsa's voice was filled with a sad loneliness.

Dallas throttled the mongoose to a stop. "Some..."

"Most?" Tulsa probed.

The tightness in Dallas's chest was crushing his lungs. Tears forced their way to the surface of his eyes and dribbled down his cheeks with abandon. "Yes, most. But what do I do? They'll know it's me and lock me in the clinker. They'll strap me then feed me to the hogs."

"There is a way," Tulsa stated. "They can read, so we will provide them with some leaflets to warn them. There is always a way to accomplish a task, if you are willing to think it through."

"What are leaflets?" Dallas asked.

"Small pieces of paper with a message on it. I'll craft a few hundred. Then, you will flying over and drop them so they flutter down over the ranch," Tulsa stated.

"I'll use the ghillie module and fly over the ranch in the evening," Dallas said.

"Splendid! There is nothing you can't think of and no problem you cannot overcome. When you land at base, I'll have a stack of warning leaflets ready for your deployment tonight."

The tightness in his chest eased, and Dallas leaned low in the saddle, throttled up his craft, and sped off toward the fallen city base.

Several weeks passed as Dallas and the others patrolled the city perimeter looking for any advanced enemy scouts. Other than a stray local or a band of deer, they saw nothing noteworthy and recorded no sign of a military advancement.

The snow dissipated, and the weather began to warm. Dallas knew that spring was not far off as they got ready to evacuate.

"When is Dirge supposed to be back?" Dallas asked Tulsa.

"Just as soon as he finishes scouting the northern ruined city," Tulsa replied. "Tommy has returned from his sky patrol. You're next, Dallas. Mount up and head south then come east and back. I've updated your Tarson Disk and flight map."

"Roger that." Dallas hustled out to his craft and mounted up for flight.

Dallas came off the tarmac and headed south. As the day got warmer, the birds were finally chirping and swooping in search of food among the treetops.

Dallas came about thirty degrees and began moving east when he noticed a column of dark black smoke rising into the sky.

He came to a stop and lowered his mongoose, settling just above the treetops, and waiting, looking all about for any nearby activity.

"Tulsa, I see smoke off toward Scatter Town," Dallas reported.

"There is active fighting occurring there. There are other flying craft. Do not engage. Return to base. I am notifying Dirge and the others." Tulsa's voice vanished.

Fear washed over Dallas. Sheela was there. He couldn't leave her. He activated his ghillie module. Both the mongoose and Dallas vanished in the sky.

He made straight for the irrigation ditch. Once down below the rim, he raced along it until he was only a hundred yards from the town's outbuildings. He armed himself with an electro-gun, crouched, and dashed across the recently plowed field.

There were other flying craft in the air. Some had pilots, and others did not. A couple of sudden blasts shook the ground. Dirt rained down over Dallas as he moved between two buildings and stopped at the corner. Here, he saw the main street. Townies with rifles and pistols were running about. Men were piling up debris as barricades at the end of the street. Others were setting up fields-of-fire positions.

"Dallas what are you doing in the town?" Tulsa asked.

"I can't leave Sheela here," Dallas said just as a man with a long gun rushed past.

The man skidded to a halt and came back, his rifle at the ready. He looked around between the structures.

"Barney, come on!" shouted another man down the street.

"I heard something," Barney called back. "But I don't see nothing." He turned and dashed away. The sound of small-arms fire filled the air.

Some women rushed past, their arms full of bandages and bandoleros of ammunition. Several carried firearms.

"Dallas, you are ordered to return to your flyer and come back to base," Tulsa said.

"Can't do that, Tulsa. I'll get airborne as soon as I can," Dallas replied.

On taking a step into the street, Dallas froze. Sheela was coming, and in her hands were two rifles and a dark beige sack.

"Sheela!" Dallas called.

She froze, looked around, and focused on the spot where Dallas was standing. "Is that you, Dallas?"

Shutting off his ghillie module, Dallas ran out, grabbed Sheela by the arm, and pulled her into the alleyway. "Stay quiet and come with me." He led her to the abandoned building.

Outside were shouts and the loud echoes of a firefight. Dallas stripped off his uniform and utility belt.

"Put this on," Dallas told her.

She set down what she was holding and put on the clothes. Dallas showed her the button to use.

"Press this and you will be very hard to see. If something happens, like we encounter soldiers or even your townies, just stay still. It is harder to see you if you stay still," Dallas said.

She pressed the switch and vanished, and then she was back. "Did I vanish?"

"Completely," Dallas said. "I've got my mongoose in the canal. We must get to it. Move low and fast. Stay right behind me." He reached over and switched the camouflage on. She vanished again.

They dashed out the door and took a sharp turn toward the fields. Commotion reigned in every direction. Dallas led the way over the rubble of the old town and into the fields.

Winged vehicles roared above, and flashes of light erupted from them as they raked the ground with fire and churned up dirt just a few yards ahead of Dallas. He cut to the left, ran a few yards, and then cut right. The flyer was making a circle.

Dallas and Sheela ran hard for the canal. From across the open field, he saw a mongoose appear and a blast of flechette rounds cut loose from its guns. The winged craft tumbled out of the sky and smashed into the ground.

There were shouts from afar. Dallas saw some men in camouflage rise from the ground fifty yards to his right. They held up rifles. Dallas stopped. Sheela ran into him, and Dallas pulled her to the ground. Projectiles flew over them. He got back up and pulled her up. Again, he made for the irrigation canal.

Ahead, Dallas saw the lip of the ditch. His feet were flying over the dirt, clumps, and ruts. Into the canal he went with Sheela behind him. His craft was just ahead, but he skidded to a halt. A man stood up with a pistol in his hand.

"Stay where you are!" the man commanded. "Put your hands up."

Dallas did as he was told. He felt quite foolish, having been caught in his underwear and olive drab shirt. The man approached. He came around the mongoose, pistol at the ready.

"Who the void are you?" the man demanded, looking Dallas up and down.

Dallas was silent.

"Turn around," the man ordered.

Dallas saw a wooden post hovering in midair behind the gunman. The man took note of Dallas's distraction and turned, only to be clubbed in the head with the post. He fell hard onto the ground and rolled into the water. The pole fell to the ground and rolled down the embankment too.

Dallas rushed down and pulled the man up onto the bank. He was still breathing but unconscious.

Sheela appeared with a broad grin. "This thing you gave me really makes the difference!"

"Come on! Put the ghillie module back on," Dallas said as he got to the mongoose and put on his helmet. In his ear, he heard Dirge call him.

"Get your ass on that ship, and let's get out of here!"

Dallas got on the mongoose. Sheela climbed on behind him and wrapped her arms around his waist. He activated the craft and took off skimming the canal. He pulled up and into the air where the woods began. The sound of gunshots echoed below. He felt something bounce off the bottom of his craft.

The fighting was vanishing behind him. Dallas made straight for the base.

"Go! Go! Go!" Dirge shouted as he appeared, came alongside, and then raced off over the treetops toward the fallen city.

Dallas followed at full speed.

Chapter 10

The Coming Storm

DALLAS' MONGOOSE TOUCHED down. Dirge was coming toward him.

"What the void are you doing in your underwear? Have you lost your mind?" Dirge shouted.

Sheela appeared. Dirge took a step back and stared.

"I couldn't leave her there," Dallas said.

Dirge's face softened. "Who is this?"

"My name is Sheela." She smiled.

Dallas removed his helmet and secured it on his craft. He climbed down and stood on the tarmac. "That's why I'm not wearing my uniform," he said to Dirge.

SHEELA SAT IN THE MESS hall. Dallas brought her some food and something hot to drink.

"So, these flying things...mongooses. They enable you to avoid the giants that guard the fallen city?" Sheela asked.

"Sort of," Dirge replied. He sat down opposite her. "This is a bit awkward. I did not anticipate a woman to come here. You can stay with us if you want, or we can try and send you back to Scatter Town."

"That is not a doable option," Tulsa said to Dirge. "The inhabitants of the town are either captured, scattered, or dead. I'm looking at the remains of the settlement even as I speak."

"I was just told that your town is no more," Dirge stated. "I'm sorry."

There was an expression of sudden realization on Sheela's face. "My mother," she said, her eyes welling up with tears. "How can the town not be there anymore?"

"There are just smoking ruins," Tulsa said to Dirge.

"The army has burned everything there. You'll have to stay here for now," Dirge told her.

Sheela sobbed. "Nothing left... My mother... What happened to her?"

"I'm sorry." Dallas put his arm around her shoulders. "She was either killed in the fighting or taken prisoner."

Sheela sat there quietly for some time. Jon brought her a fresh cup of tea. She looked at the boys and Dirge. "Alright. What do I do now?"

"Well," Dirge began, "women were not allowed in the western army when I was with it. Women were too valuable to the survival of our culture to risk. But I did read that many years before, women did fight alongside men in wars. If you want to be a ranger, I'll..." He looked at the other rangers. "We'll be happy to train you in the ways of stealth and warfare."

"A ranger? What's that?" Sheela said.

"Sort of like a sheriff-." Dallas looked over at Dirge.

"A ranger is a scout with the responsibility of maintaining an area, protect it, keep those innocents saft from marauders." Dirge leaned agains the long white counter by the food printer.

"If it means taking the fight to those bastards, sign me up." Sheela's eyes grew icy cold.

"I don't want to panic you, but there are twenty large vehicles positioned at the perimeter fence to the northeast of the city," Tulsa announced over the directional speakers in the room. "They seem to be continuously tripping the warning hologram."

"Tulsa, expand your aerial observations. Are there more vehicles and soldiers in the surrounding woodlands?"

"Not as of yet," Tulsa replied. "But once they overcome their fear or their interest in the warning message, they'll advance and most likely report back that the way is clear to enter the fallen city to their command via radio communications."

"Okay, this is the time that you"—Dirge pointed at Dallas—"Tommy, Jon, and Terry make for the northern city. I didn't find any signs of settlements up there, so you should be safe for some time. Tulsa will remain connected to you. He'll help you to further your training. Remember what you've learned here."

"What are you going to do?" Terry asked.

"First, I'm going to raze this base to the ground before those bastards get here. Then, I plan on infiltrating the army's base, finding the Old Man, and killing him. I'm sure that security will be a bit lax back at the army's main stronghold in the west." Dirge said.

"The likelihood of you being killed is incredibly high," Tulsa stated.

"I don't plan on coming back," Dirge replied. "So, the statistics are of no concern to me."

"For the record, I consider your plan to be foolish. If caught, they will torture you then execute you, as they'd planned to do originally," Tulsa reminded Dirge. "I didn't intend to save your life just to have you throw it away."

Dirge looked at the fledgling rangers, drew in a deep breath, and then exhaled. "You have your orders. Get your flyers airborne and move north."

Dallas watched Terry, Jon, and Tommy lift off to treetop level and race to the north. He turned to Dirge. "I won't forget what you did for us."

Dirge stood at attention and saluted Dallas. "It was a pleasure being a ranger with you. You're in charge now. Don't let your friends down." He turned around and went back toward the office units.

Sheela's freshly printed uniform had yet to be broken in. She pressed the ghillie module on and off and then did it again. "I can't get over how crazy this thing is." She giggled.

Dallas looked at her. "Come on. Mount up. We'll get you your own mongoose when we arrive at the northern city."

She put on her helmet, climbed up onto the saddle behind Dallas, and wrapped her arms around his waist. "I don't mind much riding like this," she said over the radio, then squeezed Dallas tightly.

A few minutes later, they were careening over the tops of the birch and poplar trees, heading north.

He looked at the speed indicator. They were traveling at top speed—three hundred miles per hour. At this rate, he'd be seeing the ruined northern city in two hours.

The flight was uneventful, and Dallas followed Tulsa's directions to the letter. Finally, they crossed the perimeter of the forgotten city, and a signal came over his radio.

"Unidentified aircraft. This space has been deemed a death zone. The deployment of RG145 is detected, and emergency warning indicators are present. Do not attempt to land." The message repeated.

Dallas took his mongoose lower as the woods gave way to urban streets and buildings. He slowed to fifty miles an hour and noted the landing zone just ahead. The military base was broad and took up most of the city center. Just north of the base was a set of massive buildings rising thousands of feet into the sky and running the complete span of the city. There'd been nothing like it in the previous cityscape. For all objective purposes, it looked like a mountain of glass and some unknown smooth material.

On bringing the mongoose down, he found where his friends had landed, and he settled beside their craft. But neither Tommy, Jon, nor Terry was to be seen.

"Where's everyone?" Sheela asked.

Dallas took off his helmet and secured it to the mongoose. "Don't have any idea." He turned on his friendlies indicator beacon. Three blips appeared a quarter mile away. "Come on. They're this way."

It took about thirty minutes to locate the others. They were in a small building with a sign that read "Officers' Club."

"What are you guys doing in here?" Dallas asked.

"Tulsa said for us to come here. He wanted us to get this." Tommy held up a thin card with a picture on it.

"What is it?" Dallas asked.

Jon shrugged. "Tulsa calls it an identification card."

"It's supposed to help us gain access to some stuff that Tulsa can't communicate with yet," Terry said.

Dallas realized that the place was paved with clothes and bones. "Let's get out of here! This place is creepy."

They all left and went to find the mess hall.

"Did you get a look at that giant building to the north?" Tommy asked.

"I did," Dallas replied. "It is terrifying in its size. If it is a building, I can't imagine what is holding it up."

SEVERAL DAYS AND NIGHTS passed. Tulsa had them busy going to buildings that had uplink systems, accessing vast complexes of offices and warehouses, and connecting the old tech with Tulsa. Once he was able, Tulsa took control of the entire base.

"I need all four of you to search the city for some items. Sheela will remain here with me. I will begin her training."

"But I want to go with the boys," Sheela protested.

"The mark of a good ranger is that she follows orders," Tulsa espoused.

She looked at the others and then cracked a smile. "Okay, I'm ready to start."

Dallas watched Sheela leave, following some flashing amber lights. "What are we looking for, Tulsa?"

"We're going to help Dirge," Tulsa said.

"What?" Dallas was surprised.

"Look, Dirge is a good man. He's walking into the maw of a dragon. The least we can do is make sure he makes his goal," Tulsa reasoned.

"But I thought you deplored killing," Dallas replied.

"I do. But under some conditions, it is appropriate. You don't know the whole story of Major Dirge Valkyrie," Tulsa said. "Has he told any of you?"

The rangers all looked at each other.

"What is it?" Dallas asked.

"The fall of these cities happened more than a hundred years ago. Afterward, fierce warring factions battled on, each seeking supremacy. Warlords made alliances, broke them, and fought on. In the devastated lands, humans tried to cobbled together a semblance of civilization, for a time. Slowly, the manpower of each army dwindled. What was left to fight for control of? Farmland? Breeding stock?

"About sixty years ago, a whole army moved west. It was commanded by a fierce warrior named Nathan Bartholomew. The man was a legend. At the battle for Droople Lochs, Commander Bartholomew singly killed eighty soldiers and commanded the slaughter of thousands." Tulsa went quiet.

"Where is Droople Lochs?" Jon asked.

"Way to the east...over what you know as the Eastern High Mountains," Tulsa replied. "shortly afterwards, Commander Bartholomew ordered his army to move west."

"What about Dirge?" Tommy asked.

"Ah, yes. Dirge was born into that world. Any able-bodied young man was put into the army at a very young age, often as young as ten years old. Dirge was bred to be an officer. All his education was focused on learning to command and lead. As he got older, he was groomed as part of their high command.

"Dirge told me that the commander had a vision of establishing an ordered civilization where the other warring factions couldn't reach. The Old Man realized that war was only going to serve the destruction of the world. But after arriving at what could only be described as a paradise, the commander began to change.

"The first several years were pleasant. The lands were rich, hectares of orchards filled with fruit and nuts, and the ground fertile for planting. Military discipline was slowly turning to self-governance. After the tenth year, the commander made an edict that there would be no civilian government and that he was the sole leader of the people. He used the army to enforce it. He ordered purges. Many were killed."

Dallas sat down, as did the others.

"Dirge was close to the commander and was to be wed to the commander's orphaned niece. Dirge was in love with her. So much was he enamored by her that he blocked out the atrocities happening just outside the main compound of the army base. Then, his love, a woman named Liana, took him out into the surrounding lands to see what her uncle was doing. Dirge was appalled. He tried to reason with the commander, but Bartholomew grew suspicious of both his niece and Dirge. In the night, security soldiers came for both. She was taken and locked up in a cell. He was taken to be killed," Tulsa paused again.

"How long until Dirge is at the enemy's main camp?" Dallas asked.

"Several days," Tulsa replied.

"So, what happened?" Tommy asked.

"He was being taken to be killed in the woods. Liana somehow escaped her captors. When she got to where Dirge was, she killed the soldiers in the firing squad and freed her lover. They were reunited but on the run.

"They escaped, but a few days later, a detachment sent to find them located where they were. Dirge was told that Liana was taken back to the base, questioned, then shot. Dirge was driven half naked, bruised, on bloodied feet to the edge of one of the abandoned cities . Perhaps it was madness that gave him the strength, but he fought one of the soldiers, took his firearm, shot two soldiers, and in the confusion, fled. That's when my scout drone came upon him. I neutralized the pursuing soldiers and established contact with Dirge by dropping a Tarson Disk to him."

"So, he's going back to avenge Liana?" Dallas asked.

"Most certainly. And we're going to help him as much as we can."

Tommy, Dallas, Terry, and Jon all looked at each other.

"So, I need you to find land mines, auto-sentries, snake traps, nerve disrupters, and laser blooms. We'll plant these along Dirge's path to help him with his task."

"Okay, I'm all in," Tommy said.

All the others agreed. Tulsa uploaded the list to their Tarson Disks, and the young rangers fanned out into the base looking for the supplies.

Chapter 11

The Old Wound

THE SPRING HEEL CRUISED above a thousand feet through the moonless night. Behind Dirge was the remains of his once comfortable home, now just shells without contents. The military base destruction system melted all the sensitive electronics, while leaving the most common elements in the event the base were to be retaken at a later date. No chance that the invaders would be able to learn any tech advancements or connect to the planetary remote sensing satellites.

Dirge looked at the scopes. Just over the horizon, and coming up fast, was a power source. From the satellite imagery he saw the expansive footprint of a typical fusion power station.

He thought about his father, his grandfather, and his great-grandfather. They all fought in the post-fall wars; their bones buried in black dirt now reoccupied by nature somewhere back east.

His father witnessed the releasing of the last nukes, sewing the ruin of the partisan holdouts by the colonial cities. In that destruction, the land armies jostled for supremacy and continued to fight well beyond the years it mattered.

It was General Bartholomew who withdrew his army from the fray. It was the Old Man who retreated into the wilderness with his war machine, technology, and his absolute command. Dirge's father was only sixteen when they moved west and founded the land they named Carpath. Shortly thereafter, Dirge came into the world.

DIRGE BROUGHT THE SPRING heel down into a thick forested area. The limbs of a half dozen old trees snapped as the mass of the aircraft came in for the landing. He switched off the hover motors and removed his crash belt.

He moved into the cargo hold, switched on a dim blue light, and then outfitted himself for his mission: travel pack, rations for two weeks, a sidearm, a rifle, a machete, and an electro-gun. He also grabbed some explosive packs and micro-mines.

He set the camouflage system to on, exited the craft, closed the rear cargo hatch, and piled brush on all sides of the spring heel. It was now virtually invisible.

After activating his ghillie module, Dirge made his way through the underbrush toward the power station. His visual implant laid out his path as Tulsa kept him informed of the enemy.

Moving was difficult. At times he used the blade to hack his way through dense briars and brush. When he encountered creeks, rivers, or ruins, Tulsa added the data to the global map. Dirge figured it was, after all, for posterity.

"I still don't understand why you didn't take a mongoose with you," Tulsa complained.

"If they find me, I'm on foot. Less tech for them to capture, and they won't readily reason I've had access to more advanced tools," Dirge replied. "I'll look like a typical scavenger."

"Makes sense, I guess," Tulsa stated. "If they think you've been in a fallen city, they will kill you."

"They'll kill me regardless," Dirge reminded Tulsa.

"I can't argue with that reasoning."

The forest ended, and a vast plain of grass extended toward the horizon. In the far distance, there were high mountains with white covered peaks. He measured how far it was to the target—another twenty-two miles.

Dirge traveled all day. By the time the sun was setting, he found a set of gullies and made camp in one . In the distance, there were howls and barking. From time to time, he saw a family of deer push their way through the tall grass. In the sky, a sliver of the red moon appeared.

He hunkered down, as the sweeping and relentless wind whistled through the swaying grass lulling him into a deep slumber. Yet, There came no dreams—just a dark and uneventful drift through a starless space.

THE SUN WAS WARMING the plain. The strong scent of the tan and green grass filled his every breath. Dirge moved steadily toward his target. After a couple of hours, he saw the metallic domes of the power complex and station. Armed men patrolled the boundary, and small unmanned security drones floated this way and that.

After stealthily inserting himself among the soldiers, he moved incredibly slowly toward the main gate. Once there, he stayed a few yards from the sentry point and waited for the guard to open the barrier.

A six-wheeled troop carrier trundled down the dirt road and halted. The guard checked the driver's documents and granted the vehicle access. Dirge slipped in behind it. Once inside, he found a concrete wall to hide behind. The soldiers he observed seemed lax and were not expecting an intruder, probably they assumed any curious locals wouldn't pose any true threat.

For hours, he searched the site, going from the cement building to the power station cooling towers. He waited at one of the access doors, and when a soldier came out, he went in. From there, gaining access into the primary power distribution center was not hard. Inside, robotic systems tended to the refurbished reactors. Here, Dirge planted some explosives.

Once done, he exfiltrated from the building and the station. He then placed micro-mines along the road. Once he armed them remotely, the small explosives would disable any vehicles that came past.

He made his way through the tall grass away from the road, then paralleled it for a time. The main body of the army was farther toward the mountains and that it would take some time to reach. So, Dirge began moving in that direction.

TOMMY SHOOK DALLAS. "Hey, do you want to come with me on aerial patrol?"

Dallas rubbed his eyes. "Sure. I'll meet you at the landing pad in twenty."

Tommy smiled. "Awesome! It's been getting sort of lonely out there these days."

Dallas grabbed his gear, got some breakfast, and found Tommy standing by his mongoose.

"What's the path?" Dallas asked.

"Tulsa has asked that we head out toward the tallest building, then come around counterclockwise toward the lake, the center parklands, then around the power towers, and back here. Should take until noon," Tommy told Dallas.

"That damned mountainous structure scares the void out of me. But, sounds like a treat," Dallas said fostering a crooked smile.

Dallas put on his helmet and connected it to the control system. He climbed onto his mongoose, fired up the hover engines, then brought the craft up to six feet off the deck. Tommy did the same.

"I'll follow you," Dallas said to Tommy.

"Catch my tail if you can!" Tommy zoomed off toward the giant building.

As they got closer, Dallas realized just how big it was. The base of the structure was enormous, spanning the entire city and then some. The depth stretched for miles, covering hundreds of city blocks. The height, like that of a mighty mountain, rose thousands of feet into the air, tapering toward the top. Below, all around the site, were garden parks, fountains, waterways, and pathways that glistened in the morning light. Around the nature spaces, other buildings of varying heights and sizes appeared like mushrooms at the base of a redwood tree.

From base to tip, the structure went higher than the mongoose was able to fly. The multi-colored surface of glass, metal, and stone-like material was entrancing, and Dallas constantly reminded himself to remain vigilant and focused on his flying.

"I'm going to take my ship up to maximum height," Dallas said and began to climb. He watched the altimeter. At one thousand feet, the craft leveled out, and he could go no higher.

He began flying around the building. Down below, he saw Tommy getting close to the side of the behemoth.

"Don't bump into it and damage your ship," Dallas warned.

"I won't," Tommy said.

"What are you looking at?" Dallas asked.

"The glass down here is shifting colors—red, blue, green, pink, purple..." Tommy stated.

Dallas came in toward the great building. The glass surface was changing colors as he looked on. He descended and then halted. He'd seen something in one of the windows. It was a face; he was sure of it.

He floated back up and stopped at the large pane of glass. It was now reflective, but he was sure that it had been translucent before. Had he seen his own reflection? Had there been a person on the other side? Now, he wasn't sure.

"How's it going up there?" Tommy asked.

"Okay. Thought I saw someone in a window, but it might have been my reflection," Dallas said.

"If you want to see inside, come down here. The windows cycle to clear every tenth color. I can see lots of stuff inside when it does."

Dallas kept looking at the window. Had it been clear before? He was unsure now.

"Okay. I'm coming down to where you are. Being up here is giving me the creeps," Dallas stated.

They puttered around the building for a while until Tulsa reminded them that they were on patrol.

"Right, Tulsa. We're continuing on now," Tommy stated. "Come on, Dallas. Let's move on."

The two friends continued along the route that Tulsa had provided. They observed lots of old and odd buildings. As they came around the park, they saw abandoned troop carriers like the ones Dallas had seen in the woods a few months before. There were other military vehicles too.

By the time the sun was overhead, they were setting down on the landing pad.

"Dallas, come to the administrative building," Tulsa ordered.

A few minutes later, Dallas was sitting in an extremely comfy green and red striped chair. "So, why separate me from the others?" he asked.

"Because I didn't want your reaction to be seen by the others," Tulsa stated.

"Okay, I'm here. Now what?"

"You did not see your reflection in that high window. There is someone in there," Tulsa told Dallas. "Let me play back your encounter."

Through Dallas's eyes, he saw the window. The movement was super slow, but it was unmistakable; there was a girl looking out as he flew past.

"So, there are people living in there?" Dallas asked.

"It would appear so. I've detected multiple power sources at that structure. Further, there are strange heat signatures within, but the density of the building makes it hard for me to see exactly what is in there. That is why I sent Tommy there. Good thing he asked you to come. It appears that the lower half of the building is not inhabited. My drones have seen no heat signatures there, but again, it is hard to measure through the wall materials."

"Someone is living in there..." Dallas mused.

"Yes, and we wouldn't have known there were people inside without your observation. The only other way we could have discovered such a thing is by sending you inside, and that would have been too dangerous."

"Do we try and communicate with them?" Dallas asked.

"Not now. Not yet. Next week, I'm sending you to where Dirge landed his spring heel. I want you to follow the path that he is taking. Use your ghillie module, and make sure you stay hidden."

"Okay, I'll start to prepare," Dallas said. He stood and headed for the door.

DIRGE WAS RIDING ON the outside of a troop transporter. The road heading west was cleared of debris, and the army was staging a great number of weapons and vehicles all along the way. Slowly, the surroundings grew more familiar. He'd spent years leading patrols and debriefing soldiers about this area. This region he knew well.

The carrier pulled over to the side of the road, and several men got out and walked around. One with captain's bars took out a case, removed a tobacco roll, and lit it.

"Another four hours and we'll be eating peach cobbler and drinking a cold beer," the captain said.

"So, what's the Old Man's goal? Are we supposed to knock down every small-time occupation along the way?" asked one of the soldiers wearing the insignia of a sergeant.

"We do what the Old Man says," the captain stated.

"Any word from our advanced scouts doing the western liberation?" the sergeant asked.

"Stalled by the pass. Radiation is still an issue out there. It's decaying, but slowly," the captain stated. He finished his smoke and tossed it into the grass. "Come on. Let's get the void out of here."

They got back into the vehicle and began moving again. Dirge remained hunkered down by the pop-up turret. Ahead, the weather was looking a bit unsettled.

The troop carrier arrived at the main base. Once inside the perimeter, Dirge waited for the craft to park and the soldiers inside to disembark.

He got down and moved to a small guard shack, around to an unlocked man door along the side of a larger building, and into a maintenance corridor.

He brought up his Tarson Disk and examined the details provided by Tulsa. The Old Man's bunker was still a few miles away. The engineers had constructed him a fortress to guard against enemies without and within.

Dirge sat back. He was behind some large pipes, and there was plenty of room to lie down if he wished to rest. On closing his eyes, he drifted off to sleep, the ambient sounds of the building gently sending him into the land of dreams.

THE FOG GREW THIN. A contingent of scouts was on his heels. Dirge ran hard, busting through brambles and thorn bushes and leaping over rushing creeks. There would be no arguing or pleading, for those who hunted him would kill him slowly for the deeds he'd done.

He stumbled across the border fence. It was rusted, overgrown in places, and leaning a bit outward in spots. He took out the multi-tool he'd stolen, and he dialed the laser down to the cutting setting. With the wave of his arm, he sliced the wire vertically.

Dirge dropped to his hands and knees, pulled the flap of chain link out, and then crawled through as fast as he could. A giant image of a man in a gray suit appeared in midair.

"Do not continue. This area is off limits. RG145 has been detected in this city. Turn back and decontaminate as soon as possible."

Without hesitation, Dirge leapt up and continued deeper into the deadly zone. A snag caught his foot, and he tumbled. Behind him, he heard tromping. He crawled into a bush, took out the tool, and prepared to use the laser as a weapon. He waited and watched the fence. Six soldiers appeared. They stopped.

"Did he go this way?" one wearing a black beret asked.

"Must have," another one said, pulling his knit cap down over his ears. He pulled up on the freshly cut fence. "This thing didn't cut itself open."

They carefully picked their way through, and then the hologram appeared again.

"Do not continue. This area is off limits. RG145 has been detected in this city. Turn back and decontaminate as soon as possible," it said.

The soldiers wavered and then slowly moved back to the fence.

"If he went this way, he's a dead man. That stuff murdered billions they say," black beret announced.

The men backed away, all the while with their eyes searching the brush on the other side of the fence.

Dirge placed the tool back into his pocket, rolled over on his back, and wiped the copious sweat from his face and eyes.

A harmonic scream rose from the soldiers. A small drone was above them, and a burst of blue lightning careened from man to man. Then, as Dirge looked on, all six of the men collapsed.

Dirge's heart raced. Would it come for him?

The thing swooped down and hovered a dozen feet up in the trees above him. He fumbled to get the tool out. Something fell from the drone. It was small, made for a human hand. He picked it up.

"I've watched you from when you escaped from that firing squad. I am making a moral choice to save your life," the thing said. "Look at the Tarson Disk. There is a map you can follow. If you wish to live, follow the course set out on the map. I will accompany you with this crude flying apparatus."

"Who are you?" Dirge asked.

"You can call me Tulsa. I'll explain more when you get to the safety of the base."

"What about the RG145?"

A chuckle erupted. "I am so glad you have given me an opportunity to use my mirthful laugh. RG145 has long since decomposed. It poses no danger to you or any other living thing."

Dirge climbed from the concealment, the Tarson Disk in his hand. He moved it around and saw the indicator light blinking.

"So, just move toward the dot?" he asked.

"Yes," Tulsa said. "I see you can think on your feet well."

DIRGE WOKE. HIS PULSE raced as he calmed himself. In his mind, the dream was not exactly what happened, but it was similar enough to evoke strong emotions. It took him a minute to remember where he was. He crawled out from behind the piping.

It took only a few minutes to place a set micro-explosive along the tubes. If he had to flee, he'd create as much chaos as possible to confuse the enemy.

A moment later, he found the exit. Once outside, he waited at the gate for something to come in or go out.

He moved to one of the roads leading west. There was a spot where any vehicle would need to slow to make the corner. He'd hop a ride from there. It didn't take long.

The transport slowed. Dirge grabbed onto the maintenance ladder and swung up onto the roof. He lay down and settled in for the ride.

Dark clouds were backing up along the high mountains. The troop transport began a hilly climb along the old road long since cleared of debris. As the vehicle approached the main gate of another outpost, Dirge held very still.

The rain was starting to come down. The perimeter soldiers looked unhappy at being pulled from their warm, comfy shack to inspect and grant access to the carrier. Following a brief exchange of pleasantries, the vehicle began moving again.

After a drive along a road bordered on both sides by high pines, the vehicle came to another checkpoint. Once the driver passed it, he parked the transport by a large cement motor-pool building, and all inhabitants of the craft got out.

Dirge waited a few minutes, then when the coast was clear, he skulked toward the main fuel depot. There he planted some micro-explosives and then headed to the administrative building.

He'd fled the madness of this army all those years ago, freed by the Old Man's niece. They'd both run, but it hadn't been far enough.

It took a half hour for him to get to the Old Man's bunker. Looking back, he saw tall smokestacks belching out black smoke in the valley. The machine of war was hard at work again. Vehicles, weapons, and armor were being churned out below. Looking back up the road, he saw the main gate of the commander's compound guarded by two soldiers. Beyond that gate was the mountain stronghold of the man he hated.

Chapter 12

Dirge the Scourge

DIRGE TOOK SOME TIME placing micro-explosives around the small fuel depot, then set traps around pathways leading down from the upper fortress. He didn't want the bodyguards and soldiers to interrupt his murder.

His movement was slow. It took him several hours to slink and crawl up to the main entrance. He scanned the area with the Tarson Disk. There was wireless communication taking place. Electrical systems were churning out RFI signals in abundance. Visual and infrared scanners were crisscrossing the open areas. Dirge was not too concerned. His uniform and face covering bent such scans around him, rendering him invisible on scopes.

He followed an officer into the building. Lots of activities were happening. Messages were being handed off to soldiers, men were issuing commands, and junior officers were rushing out the door to carry out their orders.

On coming to a stairwell, Dirge made his way up to the second floor. He waited at a locked door for someone to come out or in. The wait was not long.

Once inside, he found a boardroom with a couple of officers sitting at the table. He moved to a nook overhung by some shelves, scrunched under them, and waited.

In came a man in a wheelchair. Dirge recognized him immediately. He was older and looked worn, but it was the Old Man.

The officers sprang to their feet. The Old Man rolled up to the end of the long conference table. "Sitrep!" he ordered.

A captain spoke. "We've lost contact with two scouts who entered the city in Sector G."

"Poison?" the Old Man asked.

"Unknown. But most likely," the captain replied. "Also, our forward scout APCs are at the city border fence. They report that the message is still warning about RG145. They're waiting on orders."

"Two men lost. The possibility of poison in that city is too great. We don't want to just throw away good troops! So, we can't cross that area? We'll go around it. What news from the forward guard?"

A major stood up. "Forward units have been routing resistance in small settlements along our path. The valley will be secured once our support forces arrive. The land is rich, and the crops will be a welcome addition to the army supply chain." He sat down.

The reporting went on for some time. Dirge remembered his time in the briefing room with the commander and other officers. The Old Man was tough but seemed fair, at least to his men. But the types of actions being carried out in those days were mostly administrative: building projects, logistics, and establishing security perimeters.

"Listen, and listen good," the Old Man began. "We've built an army for a single purpose. We will rebuild civilization one conquest at a time."

Dirge moved slowly to the door that his former commander had entered through.

"I want your combat management teams kicking ass on this offensive. Competent leaders in the field at all times. Secure what we can and crush all resistance. If you must make promises that we won't keep to secure surrenders, do so!"

The Old Man rolled back, came around the table, and stopped at one officer. Dirge recognized the man—Fletcher Neil, the security mastermind of the original exodus.

"Colonel Neil, I'm trusting you to get all the intelligence we can squeeze from those country farming fops. Conscript all able-bodied boys and men. Train them up quickly. Leave no stone unturned. Also, report to me of any issues with our supply chain or our power stations." The Old Man rolled back, then turned and headed for the exit. "The colonel will take it from here," he said over his shoulder.

The door opened, and Dirge passed through with the bodyguards just behind the Old Man. Dirge followed the party of men down the hall to an elevator. They got in.

The guard pressed the button for the third floor, and up they went. The elevator stopped, and the doors opened. Dirge waited.

Once the wheelchair exited, Dirge slipped in behind it. The bodyguards stayed by the elevator, and the Old Man went down a hall and into a living space. Dirge was right behind him.

"Sully, go in the kitchen and make me some tea," the Old Man called.

"Yes, sir, commander!" said a young man who came from another hallway. He crossed the living space and went through a door.

Dirge followed the young man and jabbed him in the leg with a neuro-inhibitor. His target collapsed. Dirge caught him and eased him to the floor. He crept down a connecting hallway. It linked to the guards at the elevator. He did the same to them. They both slid down the wall to the floor.

Dirge made his way down the hallway toward the living space. He triggered the explosives at the power station. The lights went out, then the emergency lights came on.

He triggered the explosives at the refueling station, and buzzing erupted over a speaker.

"Commander, there are reports that we're under attack in Sectors Gamma and Delta," a voice called.

Dirge breeched the end of the hall. The chair and the man were gone. There was a blast, and something sticky smashed into Dirge. He tumbled back, slipped, and hit the ground.

He clawed at his face to remove some of the goop from his eyes. There sat the Old Man with a double-barrel sticky gun in his hand and a pistol in his belt.

"Who the hell are you?" the Old Man asked.

Dirge heard the elevator doors open. Several guards came into the room and leveled their machine guns at him.

"How did he get in?" one of the guards asked.

"He has a special suit that makes him hard to detect," the Old Man said. "Take him, strip him, and find out who he is and what he knows."

The two guards approached. Dirge was immobilized by the sticky goop, and his arms and legs were frozen. He was helpless.

DIRGE LAY ON THE BARE, cold concrete floor. He was now missing some fingernails, and the bruises all up and down his body kept him from finding a comfortable position. The door clanged then opened, and in wheeled the Old Man.

"Dirge, so nice of you to find your way back home. I was certain you were dead. You've aged a bit, but I guess we all have. Those items we found on you are fascinating. I read about some of them many years ago from one of the old-world tactical manuals. I never thought I'd see a working model. I'm sure as we backtrack your path, we will find more and duplicate them. Should give us an edge on conquering these savage lands."

The Old Man wheeled around the cell. He halted and looked down at Dirge. "You had great promise, son. You could have been a major or a colonel if you hadn't turned against us."

Dirge looked up as the Old Man wheeled himself toward the cell door. He stopped there and turned to face the prisoner.

"I just wanted to tell you that Liana is still alive and doing well. It is too bad that you won't see her before I have you shot." The Old Man backed up, and the cell door closed and locked.

"How the void did he know I was in his quarters?" Dirge asked just above a whisper.

He rolled over on his bruised back, then felt a hand on his shoulder.

"Tulsa says the Old Man had some special floor sensors. As you were disabling his men, he detected your movement," Dallas's voice whispered back.

Dallas flashed into view. He was crouched next to Dirge. Good thing Tulsa has those tracking things in us."

Dirge felt some strength come back into his limbs. He crawled to the wall and sat up. "You're in great danger. You must get out of here!" he pleaded in just above a whisper.

"Tulsa sent all of us. We're going to get you out of here," Dallas said.

"All?" Dirge's voice was weak. "You need to get clear of here. If they find you..."

Footsteps approached, and Dallas went invisible. There was a clang at the cell door. The door opened, and in came someone wearing a mask.

"More torture?" Dirge mumbled.

Two guards followed the masked man. Dirge knew what to expect.

The soldiers lifted Dirge by his arms and dragged him from the cold cell.

They went to a metal door down the hallway. The one wearing the mask opened it and waited for them to pass. They continued to an elevator. There, the masked torturer waited for all to enter, then he pressed the button for the basement.

"What are you doing?" one soldier asked.

"We're supposed to go to the interrogation floor," the other said.

There was a crackling sound. Both soldiers holding Dirge went limp. The man wearing the mask lifted it up. Dirge got to his knees, confused about what was happening.

"Liana?" Dirge asked weakly.

"I didn't let them kill you before, and I'll not allow it now!" she said, looking down at Dirge. She helped him up and slung his arm over her shoulder. "I have some supporters waiting at the end of the access tunnel with a carrier. We can make it at least twenty miles before my uncle knows we're gone."

Dallas appeared. Liana stifled a scream and fell back surprised.

"Don't be afraid!" Dallas said. "I'm here to help Dirge too."

She composed herself. "You... You're here to help?"

"Yes. I'm a friend and fellow ranger...like Dirge."

"Ranger?" Liana asked, confusion in her eyes.

"He's telling the truth," Dirge croaked out. His strength was failing him.

"Help me carry him," Liana ordered.

Dallas grabbed Dirge's other arm and they both supported his weight. The door to the elevator opened, and they moved out into a cement tunnel lined with dark black pipes and cables.

They moved quickly down the hall.

"That's a pretty trick you can do...suddenly appearing," Liana said.

"Dirge and Tulsa deserve the credit," Dallas said.

"Who's Tulsa? And who the void are you?" Liana asked.

"My name is Dallas." They were coming to the end of the passageway. "Tulsa is...a voice that helps us," Dallas explained.

Liana looked at Dallas. "A voice? A voice that helps you?"

"I know it sounds crazy, but Tulsa is real, and he helps us." Dallas felt his face warming.

"That's a strange story you've told me, Dallas," Liana replied as she stopped at a green door.

She helped Dirge sit against the wall. "I'll go and bring help. Sit tight. If for some reason we don't come or you hear gunfire, assume we've been captured, and do your best to get out of here and head northeast. Parallel the road some forty miles until you come to a place where the army stopped clearing the highway. From there, you'll need to head a few miles straight north. There is an abandoned depot in that area. I found it using this old map a couple years ago." She took out a paper map and unrolled it. "Somewhere along this path, if you can find it, we will meet you, provided we are not shot, captured, or killed in the process." She put her finger on a small red mark on the map.

"Dallas, I have supplied you with the location on your Tarson Disk," Tulsa said into Dallas's ear.

Dallas nodded. "Okay. I think we can find it."

Liana went through the door. Dallas activated his ghillie module, took out his electro-gun, and waited by the door.

A few minutes later, the door came open, and Liana came in with two men. They picked Dirge up and carried him up some cement stairs and out another door.

"Dallas, are you with us?" Liana asked.

"I'm here," Dallas said into her ear.

They came out onto a side road. Sitting there was a twenty-foot-long troop carrier. The rear door opened, and they all got into the back. The back door closed, and the craft came underway.

"You can unhide," Liana said.

Dallas appeared. The others were startled, but none overreacted.

"This is Dallas, a friend of Dirge's," Liana said. She kneeled and put a small pillow under Dirge's head. "I never dared to dream that you were alive."

"For a long time, I wasn't," Dirge mumbled. "My heart was broken when they told me they'd killed you. They laughed when they said it, and I was sure they'd done something terrible to you," Dirge said, his voice growing weak.

"My uncle kept me alive to marry off," she explained. "He said the human race was too important to lose a productive female."

Dirge closed his eyes, exhaled, and fell unconscious.

"Don't die on me now!" Liana ordered.

She grabbed Dirge by the shoulders and looked into his face. A moment later she reached behind her head and took down a first aid kit from the transport wall, but Dallas put his hand on hers.

"Tulsa says that I should give him this." Dallas produced a small patch from a package. He put it on Dirge's arm. "He'll recover quickly now. No need for that stuff you have there."

Liana looked on with what could only be described as slight contempt, but she did not interfere.

"You have some technology we don't have. If Dirge trusts you, I'll trust you," Liana told Dallas. "And this Tulsa."

The ride north was bumpy. The road was clear but not fully repaired or smooth. Liana went forward to the driver and then came back.

"They've discovered the escape. They're starting a search for us. We should be beyond the range for their wireless detection. Soon we'll dump and destroy the vehicle and make our way to that depot," she told Dallas.

"My comrades have set traps along the road behind us. If they try and follow us, they'll not get very far," Dallas said. "My fellow rangers will meet us at the depot too."

THE SCUTTLED TROOP carrier was now far behind them. It had taken a short time to park it deep in the woods and camouflage it with brush. Dirge regained some of his strength. It was slow going, with frequent rests, but they steadily made for the abandoned station.

"Tulsa, how far from the old depot are we?" Dallas asked.

"Three hundred yards. You will need to go in first, then connect me via the disk. I'll secure the site and then allow access for the others," Tulsa replied.

On checking the Tarson Disk, Dallas noted the amber light showing the location. "I'll need everyone to wait here," Dallas said. "I'll enter the depot first using the ghillie module. Once Tulsa has control over the place, then you can come in. I'll come and get you when it's safe."

They all stopped. Dallas vanished, and the brush shook a bit as he moved past and toward the old base.

Not worried about detection, Dallas took out his machete and cut a path toward the target. After a few minutes, he saw the outline of an ivy-covered chain-link fence topped with razor wire. He sheathed his cutting tool and found the main gate. Using his laser cutter, he opened it. Once past it, he proceeded along the path Tulsa had laid out.

The Tarson Disk gave him access to the main building. Inside was the typical deflated clothing and bones.

"Now what?" Dallas asked.

"Take the Tarson Disk to the indicated computation terminal. I will connect wirelessly. It will take a few minutes to break this code," Tulsa said.

Dallas walked around the room. There were many small tables with terminals on them. Bundles of clothing, either on the chairs or below on the floor, served as testament that no one escaped the lethal poison.

"Okay. I've got control of the site. Go and bring the others," Tulsa ordered.

Dallas followed the path he'd made. Once there, he led the others back to the depot. The smell of rain was in the air, and the evening was quickly coming. Once inside, Dallas took them to the common room, where there was a table and a bevy of chairs. He showed them where the sleeping quarters and the kitchen were, and then he came back to the common room.

"The others have arrived. They'll be here in a few minutes," Dallas said.

"Who are these other rangers you spoke of?" Liana asked.

"Friends and..." Dallas seemed lost in thought for a moment. "What's the word, Tulsa? Ah, yes...comrades. It's a new word I learned recently."

Chapter 13

Convenient Bedfellows

TOMMY, JON, TERRY, and Sheela came in. Jon went right for the kitchen, while Tommy and Terry found chairs and sat down.

Sheela came over to Dallas, hugged him, and then looked over at Liana. "I'm Sheela, and that's Tommy and Terry, and Jon is the one who went into the kitchen. You obviously know Dallas and Dirge," she said. "Who are you three?"

Jon brought out a tray with ceramic mugs, steam billowing into the cool air. There was a plate with nine pieces of toast and a bowl of jam. "Thought we all could do with a little bit of food and something hot to drink."

Everyone took some food and drink, then they sat in a semi-circle on white comfy chairs and talked.

"I'm Liana Gart. Dirge and I have known each other since the army left the deadlands of the east. This is Sergeant Van, and the other is Lieutenant Cutter." Liana sat back and balanced the mug on her knee while she took a bite of the toasted bread.

"Tulsa has told me that the sleeping spaces are open for use," Dallas stated. "He wants Dirge to stay the night in the infirmary. It's across the quad area outside. Follow the red lights in the walkway. I'll help him there. There is a small sleeper that can be set up in the medical room if you want to stay with him tonight," Dallas said to Liana.

"I will," Liana replied.

When Dirge finished his toast and tea, Liana and Dallas helped him across the walkway to a building with a red cross on it. Once inside, Dallas assisted in getting Dirge into the medical bed and then went toward the door.

"If you need anything, just say it aloud. Tulsa is listening and will reply. If there is an emergency, he will alert us. Don't worry, those coming for us have some surprises. It's unlikely they will continue after hitting our traps. Tulsa is thinking we'll have a few days if they followed us this far." Dallas exited and rejoined his friends in the common room.

Liana watched as a set of robotic arms came down and started to perform several actions at once. It stripped off what little clothing Dirge was wearing, then it applied several patches onto his arms and legs. Once that was done, a small ring moved from his head to his feet, passing a bright light over him. Then the same device passed over him again, spraying him with some mist.

Over the internal room speaker came a voice. "I have applied the repair and healing system. Dirge will be fine by morning. He will sleep well through the night. If you like, I can provide you with a patch that will make you feel calm and sleepy," Tulsa said.

"I'll be fine," Liana told Tulsa. "I'll just watch over him for a while."

"As you wish," Tulsa stated. "I don't sleep, so if you need anything or have any questions, just ask."

"Who are you, Tulsa?" Liana asked.

"I get that all the time," Tulsa said. "Think of me as an ever-present guardian angel. But I'm really a highly advanced alternate intelligence system."

"Intelligence system or not, we'll need all the guardian angels we can get once my uncle comes for us," Liana replied.

"Get some sleep. There will be much to do in the morning," Tulsa replied.

DALLAS WOKE EARLY TO the gentle coxing of Tulsa in his ear.

"The traps we set were triggered late last night. Those forces were permanently disabled. I've also searched this facility, and you should know that there are no extra vehicles at this depot. We need to airlift your companions to the northern city as soon as possible. Also, I've picked up local wireless communications from the army, and they seem quite intent on capturing you all. I've triangulated them and am tracking their movements from overhead."

Dallas got dressed and woke the others. "They're coming for us. The first group met our traps. Tulsa says we need to fly everyone to the north base. Check out your mongooses, and be ready for flight within the hour," Dallas ordered.

He went into the kitchen, where he found Van and Cutter staring at the large metal box.

"Let me help you," Dallas said. He opened a cupboard and took out a set of shiny cylinders. "This thing takes these kinds of tubes to make food." He put in the containers and then programmed the food printer to make some eggs, sausages, toast, and stim drink. "Just do what I did when you find one of these machines." Dallas went to the exit point and took out the plates of food. "Take these and put them on the mess tables."

Van and Cutter did as Dallas instructed.

Everyone but Dirge and Liana came in and ate. Once done, Dallas made two hot plates of food and took them over to the infirmary.

Dirge was up putting on some newly printed clothes. His bruises were gone, and his fingernails had regrown.

"Dallas, full marks for you and the team," Dirge told him.

Liana shifted under the covers of the sleeper. Dirge came over and sat on the edge. He put his hand on Liana and said softly, "Time to wake." There was something in his voice that Dallas had never heard before. A softness that resonated deep in Dallas's soul.

She pulled back the covers and looked on amazed. "It wasn't just a dream. You're alive," she said, rubbing the sleep from her eyes. She looked at his hands and then his arms. "You're...healed. How? I mean... We never knew such technology existed."

Dirge chuckled. "Neither did I until I met Tulsa." He stood up. "We need to get ready to go. This place is not safe, and it doesn't have the necessary resources to equip and supply all of us with what we need."

"Where are we going?" Liana asked.

"We have a base several hundred miles to the northeast from here. No radiation and only some minor issues still to be resolved. We can stay there for quite some time I think," Dirge told Liana.

She looked up into his dark eyes. "Okay. I won't be without you again. I go where you go from now on."

Dirge smiled down at her. "Dallas, let's identify who will be riding with whom and how many trips we may need to take."

"I'm on it." Dallas turned and headed out.

As Dallas passed through the door, he heard Liana ask, "This food is delicious. Who cooked it?"

Dallas crossed the quad and met up with Tommy and the others. "Okay, we need to transport everyone to the northern base."

"Dallas," Tulsa said, "I've remotely landed your mongoose with the others. With two per mongoose, you will be able to carry all but one at the same time."

"Okay," Dallas said. "I'll stay behind so Van or Cutter can be lifted away."

"So, Dirge will fly your craft. I have to tell you that staying here alone is very dangerous."

"It's the only logical answer. I have all the advantages of the ancient city folks. The new guys don't. I have ranger training, and the enemy will have a difficult time even finding me," Dallas said.

"Seems reasonable," Tulsa added. "Wait, the outpost has been scanned with LIDAR and infrared from overhead. There is a drone flying a search pattern."

"So, they know we're here," Dallas said.

"Undoubtedly," Tulsa responded.

There were multiple screeching sounds from the air. High above, flashes of light followed by explosions that cracked the cool morning air.

"We're being shelled by artillery. The compound countermeasures are destroying the shells before they can reach the ground, but it's only a matter of time before they defeat our efforts and bombs rain down all around," Tulsa said. "You have to go now!"

"What about the drone?" Dallas asked as he headed toward his flyer.

"It is flying combat patterns now, but I have a solution to mitigate it," Tulsa said.

There were several loud sounds like a powerful static crackle. A greenish craft came careering down and slammed into the trees a few hundred yards away.

"No more drone," Tulsa stated.

More ear-shattering whistles came from above, and again the base's countermeasures neutralized them before they could reach a lethal level.

Dirge and Liana came from the medical building.

"Sitrep?" Dirge ordered.

Cutter spoke up. "We're under an artillery barrage, but they're not hitting the ground."

Dallas pointed up. "Tulsa's countermeasures are protecting us. He's also set all perimeter mines for proximity detonation."

"Tulsa, trigger the explosives at the ammunition depot in the army's base." Dirge turned to the others. "We have four mongooses and nine people. I'll stay behind. Dallas, you take Liana and get her to the northern city."

"No!" Liana said.

"No," Dallas told Dirge. "You'll take my mongoose and Liana with you. I'll stay here and vanish into the woods. I'll meld into the background and be two shades darker than the void. Once you land and drop off the others, Tulsa can auto-fly back my craft. He'll know where I am."

Dirge looked at Dallas and then at Liana. He gave a weak smile and put his hand on Dallas's shoulder. "You'll be alright. Listen to Tulsa, and you'll be okay. If you get captured, we'll come and get you."

Dallas nodded. "See you in a day or so."

The shelling stopped.

"Hopefully my sabotage has bought us a few minutes," Dirge stated. "Mount up and let's get going. Your ship will be back in short order," he said to Dallas.

Dirge and the others were airborne and heading north away from the approaching enemy. Dallas ran around grabbing up supplies.

"Do you know of any safe havens within a fifteen-mile area?" Dallas asked Tulsa.

"There is a very old spaceport a dozen kilometers up the M72 highway. Know that there is no power registering at that site. If it doesn't have a working network system that I can tap into, I won't be able to manipulate anything at the location."

"It will have to do," Dallas said.

Looking back through the gate, Dallas made note of all the booby traps he'd set out. If the army of the Old Man comes, they'll have plenty of surprises waiting.

He turned and adjusted his map, then headed off toward the derelict structures that Tulsa called the spaceport.

"So, tell me again what a spaceport is?" Dallas asked Tulsa.

"Long before the fall of the cities, your kind flew into space, the region where at night you see stars in the sky."

"Why?" Dallas asked as he climbed over a dark green moss-covered fallen tree.

"Your species have an innate desire to explore. When the night comes, and if there are no clouds, I'll show you where more of your kind live," Tulsa told Dallas.

"Up there?" Dallas nodded to the sky.

"Yes. Up there," Tulsa replied.

The canopy of the forest obscured the sky as night came on. Dallas heard the roar of something over the trees.

"More scout drones scanning with radar now," Tulsa said.

"So, they know I'm here?" Dallas asked.

"The radio chatter would indicate so, though I am loath to understand how they are tracking you," Tulsa stated.

Dallas looked at his Tarson Disk. The old spaceport was only five miles to the northeast now. He rolled up his sleeve, pressed a stimulator patch onto his forearm, and then rolled it down again. "Any idea if they've penetrated the depot?"

"They seem to have bypassed it. I was able to track them by radio triangulation. They're ten miles behind you now."

Dallas pulled out a container of food, opened one end, and plunged the contents into his mouth. He tossed the tube to the side and watched it dissolve into the ground. Bugs were buzzing in his ear as a trickle of sweat dripped down his nose and fell to the ground. He stood for a moment as the stimulant kicked in.

He left the cover of the trees, looked up into the dark sky specked with twinkling lights. "How did my ancestors get all the way up there?"

"The strength of will," Tulsa stated.

"Really? What did they fly in?" Dallas asked.

"Many different kinds of ships. Ground-to-orbit ships, orbit-to-inner-solar-system haulers, interstellar ships. And, just before the collapse, intergalactic ships," Tulsa said.

"Ships? Like boats that sail on the inner seas or the ocean? Why?"

"Your species is quite strange," Tulsa added as Dallas began walking again. "They have an innate interest in learning what is just beyond their sight. Curiosity sometimes rules your species' thoughts."

Dallas felt as if he had caught his breath. He launched at a run, leaping over fallen logs, through flowing brooks, and along animal trails.

By early morning, Dallas was at a small river. He found a ford and crossed, then he came across a stone wall twenty feet high.

He stowed his Tarson Disk and scaled the structure. From on top, he saw a vast overgrown plain with what appeared to be the outline of small hills in the middle. Once down, he made his way toward the funny lumps of grass and shrubs.

His leg plunged up to the thigh into a cauldron of black water. He was in a bog, so he waded through, intent on reaching higher ground. In places there was land that came above the waterline. In the darkness, frogs croaked, and he heard what he thought was jumping fish splashing about. And mixed in with the sounds was a sulfurous peat stench.

Picking his way through, Dallas realized that the hills were buildings overgrown with foliage and moss.

The dirt piled up along the sides was a few feet thick. He began walking around looking for an opening. A place where the dirt on the roof had collapsed carved a narrow pathway under an overhang. He slipped in and found a cave where the berm did not quite meet the glass windows. A drone crossed over the hill and flew toward the west.

"Did they find me?" Dallas asked.

"No, but they are determined to."

"How do I get inside?"

"I'm searching the records that I have access to. I don't see any detailed mention of as-builds or blueprints for this site. Unfortunately, there does not appear to be any power to this area, so no wireless connections can be made. Look for a door and try the Tarson Disk. It may have a reserved power module for emergency crews to open it. If not, try to break a window."

"If they made these windows like the ones in the city, I have no chance of breaking one." Dallas continued around. The windows were black, and he couldn't see inside. The dirt that sandwiched him and the building closed in, and he could not continue circling the building. As he tried the opposite direction, he found what looked to be a door, but unfortunately, the Tarson Disk did not force it open.

"Tommy is en route now to pick you up," Tulsa announced.

"What? He's going to get himself killed! Why aren't you remote-flying it to me?" Dallas demanded.

"He insisted, and Dirge did not order him to stay," Tulsa explained. "ETA three hours and ten minutes."

Dallas made his way back to the cave opening. He scavenged brush and constructed a well-built blind at the entrance. Dark, low-hanging clouds moved in. Rain sizzled over the land, causing a cacophony of animal chirping and croaking. He remained hidden, watching, waiting.

An explosion and smoke erupted along the wall he'd climbed. As the smoke cleared, a jagged breach became visible as soldiers poured through.

The drone flew over again. Dallas retreated farther under the overhang.

"They're using a heat signature scanner. Your uniform will bend that scan around you. Be still when they arrive," Tulsa advised. "One hour and thirty-four minutes until Tommy touches down."

Chapter 14

A Dram of Misery

FROM ACROSS THE SWAMP came more than a hundred soldiers. As they approached the spaceport buildings, they set up weapons and drove stakes into the ground.

They set up sandbag bunkers and began exploring. Overhead, two drones commanded the air space, flying this way and that. Dallas remained hidden, tucked under the overhang.

"Tommy is nearly here. I'll show you on the Tarson Disk where he will land. His plan is to stay cloaked and wait for you to climb on. Once he lands, dash to where he is. I'll keep you both informed as we go."

Dallas made ready. In his eye, an amber indicator blinked. The mongoose came down silently, unnoticed by the drones or the soldiers. Tommy was only a dozen yards away.

"Now," Tulsa said.

Dallas pushed the blind aside, crouched, and rushed down the berm toward Tommy. Other than the sloshing of his boots in the mud, he made little sound as he ran for all he was worth.

"We have movement!" shouted a soldier.

"He's moving this way!" called another.

"There! A distortion!" shouted a third.

Dallas made it and leapt onto the mongoose. A blast erupted, and both he and Tommy were hit by a wire net.

"There!" a soldier called out.

A dozen armed men were coming for them. Dallas tried to get his laser cutter out. A hail of projectiles bounced against them, causing Tommy to fly off the mongoose. Dallas groped for the lifter throttle. It was too late; the soldiers fell on them, latching onto their uniforms and pulling them down.

"Hold on to 'em!" called a man who came rushing over. He connected something to the net, and a shock went through Tommy and Dallas. Both became immobilized.

"Grab 'em! Get those magic camo suits off of 'em," commanded a man in a black beret.

The net was taken off, and Dallas was roughly thrown to the ground. Binders were applied to his wrists and ankles, and he was propped up against a broken piece of cement.

"Thought you'd slip past?" the man in the beret asked. "You killed a few of my mates back there. The Old Man says to bring you back in one piece. So, we'll let the interrogators have at you once we're back. It won't be pleasant."

Tommy was set down by Dallas.

"I've alerted Dirge. Stay calm," Tulsa said to Tommy and Dallas.

"Command says to bring 'em back now. I'm taking a contingent of ten men. The rest of you stay here. See if any others are about."

The man grabbed Dallas by his undershirt and drove his fist into his face. He did the same to Tommy. Stars popped in and out of Dallas' vision.

"There. A good old rap in the face sure made me feel good," black beret said. "Okay, make 'em ready to travel!"

"TULSA HAS THEM ON SATELLITE," Dirge said to Terry, Jon, and Sheela. "Superimpose the old highways over the topographical." He took up a pointer. "Here is a bridge over a ninety-five-foot ravine. We'll plan to intercept them here." Dirge pointed. "Set up the micro-mines here and here. On the other side of the bridge, we'll set up laser blooms. That will stop any advancing unit from engaging us from that side."

Sheela was leaning forward. She focused on the battle plan. "They have flying craft. What do we do to destroy or chase them off?"

Over the topo-table was a holographic grid. "We have four scout ships." Dirge moved his hands in the air. I'll drop fifty airborne disrupters from my mongoose. They'll fly in swarms and disrupt any enemy drones by pulsing radio white noise that should disable the army's control systems. Most likely, they'll crash if they don't have emergency AI built into them."

Terry came forward. "What if I hide in this area here? As they pass, I'll lay down some mines behind them, then hit them from behind with an EMP strike."

"Okay, but remember, if they're driving in a vehicle, we need them to open one of the doors before we disable the craft," Dirge instructed. "Take extra medical supplies and ammunition. If you must ditch your mongoose, evade as long as you can. Tulsa will keep an eye on you from the heavens and report your location to a rescue team."

"You mean us. We're the rescue team," Sheela confirmed.

Dirge blinked a couple of times. "Yes, of course." He smiled at her. "Tulsa will report your situation to the others, and we'll come get you. Lethal force is approved. Those soldiers will be shooting to kill, so don't take chances." He picked up his helmet off the desk. "Meet you on the deck. We fly in twenty minutes."

DALLAS'S JAW WAS SORE. He stumbled along the path that the soldiers had cut on their way into the spaceport.

"You okay?" Tommy whispered to Dallas.

"Same as you," Dallas said. "Tulsa, can you set the mongoose to self-destruct?"

"Shut up!" ordered one of the soldiers.

Inside Dallas's ear, he heard Tulsa. "Dallas, I can communicate with your thoughts so there is no sound the enemy can hear. Just think your responses to me. I'll wait until there is a thirty-foot radial gap between the soldiers and the flyer. They seem quite interested in them right now, but by tonight, I think I can destroy it without incident."

Good. Make sure it doesn't fall into the wrong hands, Dallas thought.

"I won't let it be captured," Tulsa replied.

You heard that? Dallas thought.

"Of course. I'm connected to your brain. I can hear what you hear and see what you see and think," Tulsa stated.

I had no idea you could do that, Dallas thought.

"That's because you didn't fully understand how I work. But you've evolved a bit since first coming to us, and now, you understand much more."

Can you transfer what I think to Tommy and back again? Dallas thought.

"I can. Would you like me to?" Tulsa asked.

Yes.

"I told Tommy to not be afraid. I also told him to think his words, and I'll patch the communication between you two," Tulsa assured Dallas.

They walked in silence for two hours as they passed through the dense forest. All the while, Tommy and Dallas, with the aid of Tulsa, learned of Dirge's plan to help them escape. The bridge along the old road; that is where they would enact their plan.

What is happening in the east? Dallas thought to Tulsa.

"Not good. The army has overwhelmed all resistance. They have total control up to the Vandei River valley."

How about the place I came from—the ranch? Dallas asked.

"Occupied. It is now an advanced outpost. Many of the minders have been absorbed into the army, as have some of your older peers," Tulsa said.

Ahead was a wide clearing. They went up an incline then came out onto the overgrown road. Several dozen men were there, some smoking tobacco.

"Looks like you caught something!" a soldier with a green beret announced loudly.

"We're taking a transport," said the man who had beaten both Tommy and Dallas.

"Yes, sir," the soldier affirmed. He turned to several men sitting on the fenders. "You heard the lieutenant. Do a drive check and be ready to drive back down this mountain."

The two men jumped down, opened the falcon wing side doors, then climbed inside. The rear hatch opened, and Tommy and Dallas were shoved inside.

"Turn on the mag rail." The lieutenant put the chain up, and it stuck to the bar with a clack. "Try and get free of that, you curs!" the lieutenant said to them. "Give these boys a little candy to take the fight out of 'em. Driver, take us back to base!"

One of the men jabbed Dallas with a needle. He did the same to Tommy. It took only a few moments for Dallas' eyes to close.

Wheels rolled, and the whole craft shifted from side to side as the transport moved down along the old road.

"Can you hear me?" Tulsa asked.

No response came.

"I'll let you know when to be ready. I'm watching your vehicle from space now," Tulsa said to both Dallas and Tommy. "Your vitals are slowed. You appear to be drugged."

Still, no response.

USING THEIR GHILLIE modules, all the airborne mongoose flyers were hidden. They flew at top speed, and it took two hours to reach the gorge and bridge.

"Tulsa, where's Dallas and Tommy?" Dirge asked.

"The vehicle is forty minutes from the bridge," Tulsa responded. "There were a few places where the road was washed away. Not easy for the transport to get across. They're on the cleared road now. Traveling is more predictable."

"We'll be at the bridge in twenty. Keep a watch for enemy forces," Dirge responded.

"There is a force coming up toward the bridge from the south. They have some trailers covered in tarps," Tulsa replied. "Also, you may have to carry Tommy and Dallas from the craft. I think they've been given a sedative."

"Drugged?" Dirge asked.

"Perhaps," Tulsa said.

"How about tarps? Any ideas?" Dirge asked.

"From what you've told me of Commander Bartholomew, he's probably sent anti-aircraft equipment. Very unlikely that they can track you or lock on to you. The mongooses were designed to bend radar and lasers around them. Stay cloaked even when you pick up the prisoners," stated Tulsa.

"TEN MINUTES TO BRIDGE," Dirge said to the others. "Keep vigilant! We have a report that the enemy is coming up from the south. Terry and Jon, you fly a mile south, then deploy micro-mines to knock out whatever they're bringing this way. Sheela, you, and I will set the northern ambush and pick up Tommy and Dallas."

Each of the rangers reported that they understood. Ahead, the bridge was growing in view as they raced toward it.

"Break north," Dirge ordered, and Sheela followed him north.

"Break south," Terry said.

"Keep hidden," Dirge told them all. "Tulsa, where's our adversaries?"

"Southern group is four miles and closing. The northern group is two miles and closing. One troop carrier, no escort approaching the bridge from the north," Tulsa replied.

Dirge brought down his mongoose and landed. Sheela did the same. They quickly set out mines and distraction traps. The road was a long, straight path coming down from an incline to the bridge.

"When the transport stops, I'll open the rear door. You disable the occupants with a gas grenade," Dirge ordered Sheela.

"I'm ready," Sheela replied.

They hid on opposite sides of the road. The vehicle was now in sight and moving slowly toward them.

The troop carrier was a hundred yards and closing. Dirge went over his procedures in his mind:

Disable the vehicle, open the hatch, wait. Sheela throws grenade. Breach door and free boys.

Only fifty yards now. Dirge heard the hum of the engine as it approached. Several small blasts echoed in the hills.

"Deploy disrupters," Dirge told Tulsa.

"Executed," Tulsa replied.

Mines on either side of the vehicle blasted the carrier's wheels, tearing them from their mounts. The craft ground to a halt, its belly digging into the muddy road.

Dirge rushed in, thrust two explosives onto the hinges of the door, stepped back, and detonated them. The rear door fell to the ground.

In went the gas grenade. There was an eruption of chemical smoke. Dirge waited, then drove hard into the compartment. The two boys were not there.

Chapter 15

Fox to the Hounds

"FIRE!" SHOUTED SOMEONE.

Successive blasts careened overhead. A web of thin metal filament descended over Dirge and Sheela. Dirge retreated into the carrier. Sheela made for the edge of the netting, grabbing handfuls as she went. There was a crackling sound, and the bulge of netting that Sheela was in caused her to collapse and convulse.

Men in camouflage came from the woods and began lifting the netting and rolling it up. When they came to Sheela, they pulled her invisible form from under the netting, stripped off her uniform, and carried her to the edge of the road.

An officer in a green beret slowly walked behind the men rolling up the netting.

"Now," the officer said to a group of soldiers forming a half circle around the back of the troop carrier.

There was a bang. A splattering of blue dye exploded in the rear compartment of the carrier, leaving Dirge covered in florescent ink.

"Fire team two, stay with the female prisoner. Team one, prepare to fire on my orders. You inside the carrier, come out with your hands in the air. We will fire on you if you don't, and if you don't come out, we will throw in an incendiary grenade." The man in the beret stood at an angle to the opening.

"I'm coming out!" Dirge turned off his ghillie module and slowly emerged from the protection of the craft. He made sure his hands came out of the door first. He then waited as some soldiers came.

Two large men threw him to the ground. His hands were locked in manacles, and they pulled him up to a standing position.

The officer in the green beret came over and held up a radio handset. "Dirge, you keep surprising me." The voice of the Old Man was clear as a bell. "You didn't consider that I'd outthink you? That's why I've been in command so long. You and your friends will be taken back to the main base, and once secured there, I'll decide what to do with you all. I'll be very interested in knowing where two of my men disappeared to. I suspect my niece had something to do with that."

Green beret made no expression. "Do you want to reply?"

Dirge shook his head. "No need. I know it'll make no difference to what is going to happen."

Green beret nodded. "So true." He then addressed the men holding Dirge. "Take him across the bridge, and march him and his friend to the garrison at Venti. Secure a fresh carrier. I'll be along shortly."

They stripped Dirge down to his underclothes and took his equipment. Sheela was brought over. They were both pushed ahead of a complement of soldiers as they moved toward the bridgehead.

The sun was arching toward the horizon, and dark clouds boded rain. Watercress and cattails formed a wavy path along the wide creek that formed the estuary that the road followed. The smell of water, mint, and the other plants hung in the air heavy as the rain came.

Ahead, another group approached—Tommy and Dallas on stretchers. Up the road, a group of troop carriers and men waited. There they saw Jon and Terry.

"How did they get you?" Dirge asked.

"Metal net," Terry said.

"Shut up. Keep your mouths shut!" ordered a man with sergeant stripes.

"I'll act as messenger between you all," Tulsa said. "Unfortunately, it will take some time to bring the others back at the northern base up to speed on flying and fighting."

That's okay, Dirge thought. *Perhaps I'll get an opportunity to kill that bastard in the wheelchair.*

"More immediate concern is to keep you all alive," Tulsa said.

I suppose this was a tactical error on my part, Dirge thought.

"It would seem," Tulsa stated. "I take some of that blame as well."

DIRGE WAS STRAPPED to a table that made it impossible to look away. Commander Bartholomew wheeled into the interrogation room. He rolled around looking at the various tools of torture, then stopped for a moment and looked at Dallas, who was bloodied and unconscious.

"Still not willing to tell us where you got your intelligence?" There was a moment of silence. "Won't tell me where Liana and her coconspirators are?" The Old Man rolled over to Dirge. "If you don't start talking, I shall order my very experienced interrogators to work on your young friend here!"

Dirge was fatigued and a bit confused. The drugs they'd used on him were causing distortion in his vision. His tongue was dry from lack of water. He looked over at his young protégé and knew he could not watch Dallas be tortured.

"I think I've worked out a plan to get you all out of there," Tulsa said to Dirge. "Stay calm. Don't worry about this nonsense of physical torture. I've programmed your nanobots. None of you will feel any pain from these crude savages. Now, listen closely."

"I'm not hearing any vital information from you," the Old Man said. He turned to the faceless torturer, his mask a skull with a rictus grin. "Keep at it. Cut something off if you need to." He wheeled around and made for the door.

"Wait!" Dirge called out. "I'll tell you..."

Bartholomew turned and rolled back. "I'm waiting," he stated calmly.

"To the north, there is a fallen city. I moved our base there. From there, I was able to tap into an old satellite and watch you and your army. Liana is waiting there for me with your two deserters." Dirge tried to swallow but choked. "Water... Just a drink of water."

The Old Man examined Dirge for a moment. "Give him some water. I expect map coordinates from you. You'll tell me if there are any traps or other fighters there." He looked at one of his soldiers. "Take them both back to their cells." He rolled to the door and vanished through the doorway.

DALLAS LANDED HARD on the cold concrete floor. He curled up into a fetal position and shook from the frosty air.

"Dallas!" called Dirge from the other cell. "Stay alive! Don't die now."

There was silence.

"Dallas, can you hear me?" Dirge called.

"Yes, he hears you," Tulsa replied. "But he is quite incapable of speaking at the moment."

"Keep me informed on his vitals," Dirge ordered.

"Quiet down there!" shouted a guard.

"Be careful, Dirge. Don't give away the store," Tulsa said. "Use your thoughts, not voice."

Can't give away the store since you're the grocer, Dirge thought.

"That's quite funny," Tulsa said into Dirge's ear.

Dirge crawled to the wall, sat with his back against it, and stared at the cell door. "It's only a matter of time," he whispered.

The door rattled, swung open, and slammed into the wall. "Wake up!" shouted a guard as he dashed a bucket of cold water over Dirge.

Dirge struggled to get to a kneeling position. The guard put manacles on his wrists. Then a second captor came in, and they both dragged the prisoner from the cell.

Ahead was the door to the interrogation room, but they passed it. At the end of the hall, one of the guards pushed a metal door open. Bright sunlight blasted into Dirge's eyes, blinding him.

Across the compound they carried him until they entered another building. Dirge was tossed into a cold steel chair by a metal table, and his handcuffs were secured to a ring attached to it. The opposite door was opened, and in came the Old Man.

"You don't look too worse for wear," Commander Bartholomew said. "We've sweated your other... What do you call your little group of agitators? Ah, yes. Rangers. We know there are only six of you, and I have six in custody."

Dirge remained quiet.

"I've given it a lot of thought. If you help guide us to where Liana and her traitorous friends are, I might persuade the other officers to spare your life. Maybe even let you and Liana leave here. How about a small homestead somewhere within the confines of my new empire? It might be arranged."

"And all I have to do is take your men to the northern base?" Dirge asked.

"Yes," Commander Bartholomew stated.

"Betray the woman I love?" Dirge challenged.

"Either that or I have your rangers tortured in front of you then have you shot. If this base is as advanced as you make it appear, I need someone to guide me around it. You have some bargaining clout here, son. I suggest you take advantage of it."

"Once I lead you to the northern base, you let Liana and I go," Dirge pressed.

Bartholomew looked deep in thought. "Of course. Why not? She's been a pain the ass every day since you and she became romantic. In fact, I'll let you and your whole little band of miscreants go free. That is, of course, if you all promise not to interfere with my expansion. Oh, and your friends will stay here in case you have some tricks planned for us on the trip." The Old Man turned and paused. "Yes? No? I'm waiting."

"Us?" Dirge asked.

"I'm coming with you, escorted by my security team and some assault troops.

"Okay. You hold all the cards anyway. Why the void not?"

Bartholomew said over his shoulder, "Make him ready for travel." He then rolled out of the room.

DIRGE WAS IN FAMILIAR attire—the typical uniform of an east army soldier with its shifting camouflage pattern. It fit a bit loose but was comfortable.

He was escorted out to a velo-copter sitting on a concrete flight pad. Several well-armed squads were standing by, ready to mount into other copters. The Old Man was rolled out to one of the flyers, and with assistance, he climbed into the copilot seat. Dirge was shuffled into the craft and handcuffed to a metal loop by the jump seat.

An escort soldier sat next to Dirge. "We'll be in the air for five hours before we reach the location you gave us. I really hope you didn't fuck us around, or I'll personally throw you out of this copter from ten thousand feet," the officer said.

The craft lifted off and rose. Dirge watched out the alumina windows as the Old Man's citadel grew smaller below them. The craft began moving forward as the other aircraft flew in formation alongside them.

DALLAS MOVED HIS ARM out from under his body with great effort. There were burn marks where the interrogators had attached the electrodes.

He'd been tortured, but the agony was muted. Tulsa explained the process of pain blocking, but Dallas really didn't understand it. He'd expected at least the same crippling pain he'd experienced during his time at the ranch. He struggled to sit up. The water dish was not far.

He crawled to it and took in the revitalizing liquid. His throat and tongue were as dry as desert sand.

Outside the cell door, he heard the rap of boots on cement.

"Soldier! You're relieved. This is one of the new recruits," someone said.

"What's the challenge?" one of the soldiers asked.

"Bravo Orange," said a familiar voice.

"Delta Black," the other soldier replied.

"I'm here," the familiar voice began, "to learn the tasks of a base-central soldier."

"Follow orders, and don't deviate from protocol. You'll do fine," said one of the soldiers. "Group 154 soldier relieved!"

Dallas crawled toward the door and leaned against its bars. The hallway outside was dimly illuminated by overhead lights.

His cell was dark. The coldness of the concrete floor stung his skin as he looked hard into the hallway past the cell door. The new guard was a young man a little older than he.

"What's your name?" Dallas mumbled through swollen lips.

The soldier kept staring straight ahead at the wall. "William."

"William from the ranch?" Dallas asked.

The soldier slowly turned to look at Dallas. "Who are you?"

"It's me...Dallas!"

"Dallas?" William said surprised.

"Yes, it's me. I'm a bit beat up now, but it's me."

William smiled, and the tops of his upper teeth showed. "It is you! At the ranch, that son of a bitch Burk told us that you were killed trying to run away. That was before the army came and took all of us."

"I can't believe it's you," Dallas said. "God sure is a funny bloke."

"What are you doing in there?" William asked.

"Tommy, Terry and Jon are in here too," Dallas told William.

"Soldier!" shouted a voice from down the hallway. "Come and assist. We're moving this prisoner."

William looked down the hall and shouted. "Right away, sir." Then he looked back at Dallas. "I'll be back."

Tulsa, Dallas thought.

"I'm here," Tulsa said in Dallas's ear.

A friend of mine is here as a soldier. He might be willing to help us, Dallas said in his mind.

"Really?" Tulsa replied. "That is one of the most improbable things I've ever heard. I'm going to formulate a plan. Don't worry about informing me. I'll be listening and seeing everything that happens with you and the others. Do your best to convince him to help."

A few minutes passed, and William came back down the hall.

"They're planning to kill us," Dallas said.

"Not while I'm around," William told him. "Listen, I'm going to get you all out of here. Just be patient. I'm the lowest of the low here now. They can order me anywhere at a whim. So, we'll have to play this by ear."

"Just knowing you're going to help lifts my heart," Dallas said.

"Don't get all mushy on me, Dal," William replied with a smile.

For several hours, Dallas and William whispered between the bars. Slowly, Tulsa's plan was laid out. William knew several other young men who had been plucked from the ranches of the fertile valley region.

"Dallas?" said Tulsa.

"Yes," Dallas whispered.

"I need to tell you that Dirge is near the northern base. Here is how this will all play out for you there. I will fly a spring heel directly to you. At full speed, it will take forty minutes to reach your location. Be ready to escape. You and the others will need to get to the courtyard just outside the prison cellblock. When I land it, the rear gate will be down. Run for the flyer, and don't leave anyone behind."

"We'll do our best," Dallas whispered.

"You'll have to if you intend on living past today," Tulsa stated.

"What about Dirge?"

"That remains to be a gamble," Tulsa said.

Chapter 16

Liquid Sky

THE SQUADRON OF AIRCRAFT came down into the fallen northern city. The skids hit the ground, and the doors were thrown open. Dirge was pushed out and away from the craft.

The Old Man was helped down and put into his wheelchair.

"So, all this time the RG145 was no longer a danger." He chuckled. "Come on, son. Time to earn your freedom!" Bartholomew shouted.

A squad moved ahead to ascertain the safety of the area. The main force waited.

Another squad went around the landing zone, driving in stakes.

"What are they doing?" Dirge asked.

"Seismic sensors," one of the soldiers said. "Even though your confederates might be invisible, you still had to walk on the ground!"

Did you hear that? Dirge thought.

"I'd suspected," Tulsa replied. "Your commander is a smart man."

I hope we're smarter, Dirge said.

"Relax. All is in order," Tulsa said with confidence.

"Come on. Bring the traitor. You'll show us to your hideout and the others," the Old Man called.

Dirge came forward and stood beside Bartholomew.

"Stay close. Your friends are less likely to try and kill us if you're in the middle," the Old Man stated.

They walked for a few minutes, and then the main gate of the military base came into view. The swirling razor wire ran along the top of the fencing, stopped only by the gap between the two large gates and the guard stations.

"Now, what's the trick to getting in?" the Old Man asked.

"All I have to do is approach. Once we're inside, you can be equipped with the digital signatures that will allow you to own this fortress," Dirge told the Old Man.

Bartholomew cracked a smile. "Good to know. Perhaps you might find your way back into my good graces yet."

Dirge did not reply but instead glanced along the fence. In the distance, the mighty glass arcology dominated the skyline.

"Go with him," the Old Man ordered two of his soldiers. "We'll wait here for the gate to open."

Dirge approached. A red light on top of the gate started to flash, and the door slid open. Dirge looked back. "Are you coming?" he asked.

The others came forward, and all entered the base.

"WE HAVE ORDERS TO TAKE the prisoners out to the eastern wall and shoot them," a young man with a lieutenant's bar said to William.

Four soldiers accompanied the officer. William looked at the order and nodded. He removed the key card from his belt and opened the cell door. Two soldiers entered and dragged Dallas out into the hall.

Down the hall they went, extracting Tommy, Jon, Terry, and Sheela. Two guards walked in front and two in the back, followed by the lieutenant. On exiting the cellblock, they walked around to the east to a thirty-foot-high cement wall. There, all five were lined up with their backs against the wall's pockmarked surface.

William checked the timer on his comm readout and left his post in the cellblock. Outside, he turned right and headed east around the building. There he saw his friends lined up against the wall and the soldiers standing, rifles in hand.

"Stand at the ready!" shouted the lieutenant.

The soldiers brought their rifles up to bear.

Several other young men from the ranch came and stood next to William.

"Wait!" called William as he ran up to the lieutenant. "You dropped this at the cell," he told the officer while holding an ID card out.

Looking annoyed, the lieutenant drew in a deep breath, exhaled, and walked over. "What is it?" he demanded.

William handed him the item. The lieutenant examined the identification. "This is your ID card," the lieutenant said with annoyed venom.

William drew his pistol and fired point-blank. The officer went down bloodied. William kneeled and fired at each of the riflemen who were frozen in shocked at what was happening.

The other boys from the ranch fired too. Each of the men in the rifle squad fell as William and his friends placed their deadly shots with a hunter's accuracy. When none of the enemies were standing, William holstered his weapon. He rushed to Tommy and freed him of his bonds. He did the same for the others.

There was a loud crack in the sky. The spring heel came out of ghillie mode, slowed, and descended quickly. The craft landed softly; the rear hatch was open like the mouth of some large monster.

Several soldiers rounded the corner of the cellblock and began shouting. Small-arms fire erupted, and projectiles bounced off the skin of the spring heel.

Tommy stood at the hatch shoving each escapee into the craft as they came past. The door was coming up, and the ship lifted rapidly skyward. Everyone inside was thrown to the floor. William stumbled into the passenger area.

"Secure yourselves with crash belts. I'm moving into supersonic speed in twenty, nineteen, eighteen..." Tulsa said.

"Sit in a chair!" Dallas shouted at everyone. "Take this strap, and secure it like this."

William did. His hand came back with blood on it. He looked at the red fluid with some confusion, wiped his hand on his uniform blouse, and settled back.

The cabin shuddered, and everyone was pressed back into their seats.

"Do you want me to make the hull clear so you can see the world around you?" Tulsa asked.

"No!" shouted Dallas.

BLACK THUNDERHEADS were heading toward the city. Long tendrils hung from the sky, foretelling the approach of showers. Now and again, golden beams of sunlight pierced gashes in the clouds and swept over the cityscape.

"Where to, Dirge my boy?" the Old Man asked.

"There." Dirge pointed at a distant array of large buildings.

"Scouts, take a look and report back," the Old Man ordered. He shifted in his wheelchair and looked at one of the officers with the group. "Send the tech team around, and document the things that look tactically beneficial."

"You'll find plenty," Dirge said.

"Something seems to be interfering with our wireless," a young soldier stated.

"Find the source and knock it out," one of the officers ordered.

A soldier removed a tracking device and began pointing it at various buildings.

Dirge was quiet. He just watched as the men moved farther afield.

"Everything is in position," Tulsa said in Dirge's ear.

Good to hear, Dirge thought.

"Scouts are almost to the far buildings," an officer with binoculars said to Bartholomew.

The Old Man drew in a deep breath and exhaled slowly. "Okay, let's close the distance."

They began moving toward the structures. Dirge was in front, and the Old Man was next to him.

From his holster, Bartholomew drew his pistol. "If there is any shooting, I'll kill you first," he declared.

"I wouldn't have it any other way," Dirge quipped.

He glanced down at the Old Man. Bartholomew's eyes narrowed.

"They've penetrated the exterior," the officer with the binoculars said.

A few minutes passed, and the Old Man halted the group. "We wait here," he told them. "Place the stakes around."

From the large buildings emerged one of the scouts. He waved his hand in the air, gestured to a gap in a large open hangar door, and then went back into the darkness of the building.

"Close your eyes tightly," Tulsa said.

Dirge did so and covered his eyes with his hand.

He felt the blast of light on his skin. There was a cry of confusion from the armed soldiers. Dirge dropped his hand and ran for the old hangars. Several shots rang out, but he kept sprinting.

In the sky, a crack of thunder echoed. Dirge made it to a broken chunk of concrete wall and dove behind it. He quickly peeked over. The Old Man was being wheeled back toward the velo-copters.

A boom echoed as a spring heel appeared overhead and came down.

Flying craft came from the gigantic arcology. They converged on the remaining soldiers of the army, blasting them with a thick, sticky foam. The Old Man's soldiers attempted to escape, but most of them were tangled in the gooey stratum.

Liana rushed from the hangar. She came to a halt by Dirge and used the Tarson Disk to disconnect the shackles around his wrists. The metal clamps fell to the ground. She shoved a rifle into his arms.

"Come on!" she shouted as she pulled him toward the hangar doors.

BARTHOLOMEW HAD ALMOST reached the velo-copters when a flying craft that looked like a more advanced version of the mongoose fired bright beams of light. The copters and pilots were destroyed instantly. The two soldiers with the Old Man stopped, whirled around, and headed toward a series of cement conduit structures. The men dashed into the concrete tunnels without a backward glance.

Once inside, a bodyguard ignited a flare and led the way deep into the tunnel. The Old Man fumbled with his belt, pulled forth his radio comm, and pressed the transmit button.

"Under attack at these coordinates," Bartholomew said and pressed a GPS button on the transmitter.

"Sir, if they did not knock out that interference, that transmission won't reach our troops," one of the bodyguards said.

"What the hell else should we do?" the Old Man asked. "It's worth the attempt. Now find us a place we can defend, and then find a way out of here."

"We can't separate, sir. Our duty is to keep you alive now," the other bodyguard said.

They came to a bifurcation.

"Which way?" asked the lead bodyguard.

Bartholomew thought for a moment then pointed. "That way. I feel a draft from there."

They went down the left tunnel as fast as the wheelchair could go. The smell of mildew and rot was strong. Still pools of black water and rotting vegetation became plentiful. Looking down, the Old Man realized that they were in a drainage system, and water was beginning to move. They came to a ten-foot-high wall. Both men pushed Bartholomew up, then one climbed up and the other handed up the wheelchair.

"Come on!" the Old Man said.

The bodyguard climbed up, and the soldiers got Bartholomew back into his chair. Again, they moved along the cold passageway.

DALLAS JUMPED FROM the rear hatch of the spring heel. In his hands was a plasma pulse rifle. Small-arms fire erupted, and projectiles pinged off the hull of the flyer.

"Get to the barracks. I have a fresh uniform and equipment for you," Tulsa said. "Don't worry about your friend William. I'll see to his wounds."

"Where's that bastard the Old Man?" Dallas asked, his blood boiling.

"He and two men have vanished into the northwest drainage tunnels," Tulsa replied.

"Where does it lead?" Dallas asked.

"There is an old hydro-electric management complex two point six miles upstream. To pursue them is not wise," Tulsa cautioned.

Dallas looked over at his friends and then sprinted to the barracks. He jammed his legs into his trousers and put on his battle fatigue blouse. He secured his utility belt and ghillie module, grabbed some extra weapons, and ran out the door.

Outside he found one of the spare mongooses and put the helmet on. He climbed onboard and activated the hover engines.

"Going alone is not advisable," Tulsa repeated.

"I'm not letting that son of a bitch go. Not after what he did to all of us!" Dallas said into his helmet mic.

"Very well. I've laid out a course for you. Follow it. Your fate awaits you," Tulsa stated.

THE DANK HYDRO-POWER plant lay in ruins. The ancient dynamos were rusted and damaged in places. The Old Man rolled toward a hallway. He stopped and ordered his men to stand guard while he checked further.

A few dozen yards in, the hallway widened into what must have once been a work area. Dilapidated machinery rusted and lay wet in the darkness. From the side of his wheelchair, Bartholomew pulled a machine gun and set it in his lap.

As he searched the room, he saw places in the roof that were cracked and jagged, with rusted metal protruding. Rain dripped down, filling puddles on the floor, and thunder cracked in the distance.

Down the hall, he heard one of his men call to the other.

"Look there! Something moved."

A burst of fire echoed down the hallway, and projectiles spun off the concrete.

"Over there!" called the other bodyguard.

More small-arms fire.

The Old Man heard a heavy thud against the ground and then another. He switched on his infrared miniscope and focused it down the hallway. Only his bodyguard's red glowing flare showed. Bartholomew pulled back the bolt on the upper receiver of his weapon, leveled the gun down the hall, and fired a burst.

The projectiles flashed off the walls as they raced away into the darkness.

"You missed me," Dallas's voice called out from somewhere close.

The Old Man fired again in the direction of the voice.

Dallas's voice now reflected from all around. "I thought you were a great commander. You're slipping, old man."

Bartholomew fired again, then the bolt slammed shut on an empty chamber. He jammed another magazine into the weapon and cycled it. Another short burst and the gun was empty. He pulled out his pistol and fired down the hallway. Bullets flashed around the room as sparks and aging concrete flew in all directions. The Old Man rolled back and then hit some broken pipes that stopped his movement.

"Come out and fight me!" the Old Man shouted. "Your avoidance mocks me!"

DALLAS DECLOAKED. IN front and down the dark hallway was the Old Man, holding a pistol leveled at Dallas. The thick cement walls, puddles of water, dark interior, and constant dripping made Dallas feel as if he were in a cave.

"Goodbye, boy," said the Old Man.

There was a loud click. No bullets left in the pistol.

Dallas pulled forth his combat knife and slowly approached. This man had his friends tortured...murdered hundreds if not thousands.

Dallas stood over the wreck of a man. He took the gun away and tossed it to the side. There was contempt in the Old Man's eyes, a defiance seen only in strong men of conviction who were about to die.

"Do it, boy," the Old Man said from his wheelchair. He tore his shirt open and tossed his head back. "Drive that knife right in there. Or do you lack the will of a fighting man?"

A thick and purple vertical scar ran down the Old Man's chest between the many old bullet wounds from long-past battles.

Dallas's blood was cooling, the fire-hot rage only now simmering. His rational mind was coming back under control.

"I'm the one who ordered you all executed! And if you don't kill me, I'll see that girl you like is raped in front of you!" the Old Man said. "I'll rape her myself."

Dallas examined the Old Man's eyes. He realized that the leader of the eastern army was baiting him hard.

Sheathing the knife, Dallas shook his head. "Not today! I don't take orders from you. I hope you live another twenty years. I hope that with every waking breath and in every dream, you relive this moment. Where someone like me let you live."

"You're weak! You'll never make it out of this city. I'll see you fed to the hogs while alive!" the Old Man yelled.

Dallas searched the Old Man for any other weapons. Nothing. He kicked the machine gun away and into a hole in the wall, tossed the pistol down the hallway, and turned his back on the Old Man. He then walked past the unconscious bodyguards and into the darkness of the cement tunnel.

As Dallas walked toward the broken turbines, a shot rang out. He turned and crouched. There was nothing but darkness in the tunnel. He raised his rifle and took a knee. He saw the air shimmer.

"Dirge?" Dallas called.

Dirge, bloodied and bruised, came into stark focus. He looked down at the two soldiers lying unconscious on the ground.

"The Old Man?" Dallas asked.

Dirge shook his head. "That was old business. Now it's settled." He pointed his pistol at one of the soldiers lying below him.

Dallas came and put his hand on Dirge's arm. "A wise man once told me to refrain from murder," Dallas said. "No worse weight a man can carry in his heart than the murder of another person."

Dirge looked over at Dallas. A soft chuckle escaped his lips. "I think I heard that before." He nodded at Dallas and smiled. "Come on," he said. "Let's get back over to the base. The enemy is routed, and we've captured some of the Old Man's men." He started walking toward the exit. "You know, Dallas, you've become pretty wise hanging around me."

Dallas laughed. "Since I met you, I've never been so close to being killed. It makes a boy wise."

"A man wise," Dirge corrected.

Dallas smiled.

"Tulsa, any suggestions regarding the bodyguards I left alive?" Dirge asked.

"I have marked the men for pickup and incarceration."

"Incarceration?" Dirge said.

"In a manner of speaking," Tulsa replied.

They exited the old power station and went to their respective mongooses. Each lofted into the air. The way back to the base was empty of enemies; only a swarm of dark black birds shifted in the cloudy sky over the city.

"Now what?" Dallas asked into his comm.

"You're both lucky to be alive. Neither of you listen well!" Tulsa chided. "Well, at least you're all going to grow a little older."

"What did you mean when you said incarceration?" Dallas said.

"The city dwellers will seize the enemy soldiers and lock them up for now," Tulsa said.

"What will become of them?" Dallas pressed.

"Those in the archology may let them live with them, or they have tech to modify their memories. They might send them home to the eastern army with no memory of their experience here today. Either way, no harm will come to them...serious harm, I mean," Tulsa stated.

"Don't they now know the poison in the cities is gone?" Dallas' voice was earnest.

There was a strange sound Tulsa made, as if he was deep in thought. "Yes. I suspect there will be more exploration of ancient places when the truth spreads. And since the Old Man is dead, the iron grip he held over the army of the east will cause it to fracture. Some of the soldiers will drift away, some will settle in the lands they ravaged, and others will probably become a protective force in the valley."

DIRGE APPROACHED THE representative of the arcology. She was tall with long black hair that fell to her shoulders. She wore clothing with odd patterns that changed color every few seconds.

"Your friend Tulsa has told us something about you all," she said with a smile.

"The Tarson Disk that your comrades delivered to us has allowed our adaptive neural net to connect to him. He has generously offered his database for our use. We have a record of your experiences and travels now.

"Many of us from the tower were living when the fall of the cities came. We've watched the devolution and rebirth of civilization from those lofty heights for many years." She watched them like a mother does her youngest children.

"Thank you for your help," Dirge stated.

"We are pleased that we could help you. The full credit goes to Tulsa, though. Without his intervention, we would have only observed." She looked back at several other tower dwellers. "It has not been our habit to interfere with the goings-on of those that live beyond the city boundaries."

Dirge spoke. "Several of us want to take advantage of your offer to stay with you in the tower. And a few of us want to try for another city further to the west."

"Those who wish to stay are welcome. Those who wish to leave may go," the woman said.

DALLAS, SHEELA, TOMMY, Jon, and Terry went to their respective mongooses.

"I'm going to miss you, Dirge. You were more a father to me than I've ever known." Dallas fought back tears.

"We'll be in touch." Dirge said with a grin.

Dallas wiped his eyes with his fingers. "I'll let you know when we've landed and when we have Tulsa in control of the northwest military base. I hope you and Liana make a home here."

Dirge nodded. "It was time for me to stop roaming the landscape," he said. "Tulsa will keep us connected. If you have any question, all you have to do is call my name."

"So, is this the end of the rangers?" Dallas asked his mentor.

"That's up to you all," Dirge said. "My time is done."

Dirge and Liana turned and began walking toward the massive mountain of metal and glass. Dallas watched them for a time, his heart heavy. He turned to his friends.

"Mount up. Daylight is burning down."

Dallas, Sheela, Tommy, Jon, and Terry lifted off. At one hundred feet, Dallas turned his craft toward the west, signaled to his mates, and engaged the forward momentum drive. The craft raced off toward the high mountains and the retreating sun.

Don't miss out!

Visit the website below and you can sign up to receive emails whenever Lawrence BoarerPitchford publishes a new book. There's no charge and no obligation.

https://books2read.com/r/B-A-MRTR-DEUYC

BOOKS 2 READ

Connecting independent readers to independent writers.

Did you love *The Leftover World*? Then you should read *Goblins, Dames, Booze & Bullets*[1] by Lawrence BoarerPitchford!

[2]

Black magic: Goblins: Mystery.

In the filthy and corrupt metropolis of New Gate, Max Draber offers his detective services to the elite and the unsavory.

---

1. https://books2read.com/u/49aGnX

2. https://books2read.com/u/49aGnX

Once an effective constable he had worn the bronze badge with pride. But after working in the city's slum of Goblin Town, his moral compass took a beating. Like a wayward soul, he now makes his living now off the underbelly of the cold city streets. When a young goblin woman is murdered on his doorstep, Max is launched into a tumble straight at New Gate's depraved world of politics, ruthless mobsters, and black-market magic.

Will Max be redeemed, or will he spiral deeper into the evils of Goblin Town?

Read more at https://www.boarerpitchford.com.

About the Author

Author Lawrence BoarerPitchford creates and publishes fiction in many genres. From humble beginnings to worldwide author, Lawrence has carved out a niche in the area of fictional works. Barbarian fantasy, classic fantasy, science fiction, historical fiction, and horror/thriller, he has created many memorable worlds, characters, and stories.

Read more at https://www.boarerpitchford.com.